Violets
Amazing
Summer

Violet's Amazing Summer

BOOK TWO
of the
*A Life of Faith:
Violet Travilla*
Series

Based on the characters by
Martha Finley

MCP
Mission City Press
Franklin, Tennessee

For a FREE catalog call 1-800-840-2641.

Library of Congress Catalog Card Number: 2002103833
Finley, Martha
        Violet's Amazing Summer
        Book Two of the *A Life of Faith: Violet Travilla* Series
        Hardcover: ISBN 10: 1-928749-18-6
                          ISBN 13: 978-1-928749-18-9
        Softcover: ISBN 10: 1-934306-02-9
                          ISBN 13: 978-1-934306-02-4

Printed in the United States of America
4 5 6 7 8 9 10 11 — 11 10 09 08 07

— FOREWORD —

At Ion plantation, more than a year has passed since the tragic death of Edward Travilla, and the family is moving on with life, supported by their faith and the knowledge that they will all be united again when God calls them home. The loss has been particularly hard for Violet Travilla, but she has learned to be inspired by her father's example of Christian love and compassion. At the opening of *Violet's Amazing Summer,* the second installment of the *A Life of Faith: Violet Travilla* series, she receives a surprise invitation that will lead her to new places, new people, and new opportunities to help others in unexpected ways.

The Violet books continue the saga of Elsie Dinsmore Travilla and her children—a story that spanned twenty-eight novels written in the nineteenth century by Miss Martha Finley, a remarkable woman and a pioneer in the field of Christian literature for young people. Although the original books have been carefully adapted by Mission City Press for today's readers, every effort has been made to honor her commitment to provide readers with models of unshakable faith.

Violet's Amazing Summer will take readers into the life of a teenager of the Victorian age. It is a time very different from our own. But readers will soon discover that Violet also has much in common with today's girls and young women as she faces unexpected challenges and sets off on new adventures with faith and love in her heart.

v

∽ MANNERS IN THE VICTORIAN AGE ∽

The Victorian period takes its name from Queen Victoria, who ruled England and the British Empire from 1837 to her death, at age eighty-one, in 1901. She was the perfect model of Christian faith, moral character, devotion to family and country, and exemplary personal behavior. Victorian ideals of proper conduct and social manners quickly spread to America, where they were adopted and adapted, particularly by the wealthy and the growing middle-class.

The United States didn't have the social system that was traditional in England and Europe. Americans were not divided into classes based on the circumstances of their births. Nineteenth-century Americans were proud of their democratic spirit. Still, they were not above drawing distinctions among themselves.

A few American men were amassing great fortunes as the country became industrialized in the 1800s. The owners of railroads, shipping companies, factories and mines wanted to distinguish themselves from everyone else. So they looked to England for the model of social separation. They couldn't take royal titles, but they did copy the manners of aristocrats. They built palatial mansions, employed dozens of servants, spent lavishly on entertaining and travel, and transformed English manners into the most complicated etiquette system Americans have ever known.

The lifestyles and activities of the wealthy were widely reported in newspapers and magazines. Average Americans who had achieved some level of material comfort demanded etiquette guides. Some people were snobs and social climbers. But most Americans tempered formal etiquette with large doses of common sense, fairness, and practicality. Even on

Foreword

America's western frontier, practical people regarded good manners as ways to put the Golden Rule into practice and to show respect and consideration for friends and strangers alike.

∽ WHAT IS ETIQUETTE? ∽

Centuries ago, in the French royal courts, an *etiquette* was a notice describing correct forms for court ceremonies. Later, the term was applied to actual behavior in social situations, and the English borrowed this meaning of the word.

Today, "etiquette" covers not just behavior on special occasions but the rules of polite behavior in everyday life. When you chew food with your mouth closed or stand up for an older person who enters the room, your good manners are examples of correct etiquette.

Victorian manners can now seem very stuffy and restrictive, but they suited the needs of that era. The following sections will give you an idea of the rules and conventions that mattered to people in Victorian times.

∽ THE ETIQUETTE OF CALLING ∽

The Victorians regarded "calling"—making and receiving social visits—as a fundamental part of everyday life. Women called on other women and married couples—but never visited a man except for professional reasons, such as seeing one's doctor, or when the man was an invalid. When men called on other men, their meetings were likely to be much more easygoing than when ladies were present.

Usually around age eighteen, young women could receive callers on their own. Before a man could court a young lady, he had to get her father's permission. Although a man might call on an unmarried woman for reasons other than romance, a chaperone would be present or close by, unless the man and woman were related.

Calling cards. When arriving at someone's home, the well-mannered Victorian would present a calling card, or visiting card, to whoever opened the door. Calling cards were provided even if the caller had been specially invited to visit.

The calling card—a small, plain white card engraved with the person's name—was taken to the lady or gentleman of the house, if she or he was at home. The visitor might be invited in. But if the visitor was told that "Mrs. Jones is not at home," it might mean that she was literally away or that she was there but it was not a convenient time to visit. Victorians weren't offended to be told someone was "not at home" even when they knew the person was really in the next room.

A corner of the card might be folded over as a message. If the upper left corner was bent, the caller was only visiting; a folded upper right corner meant congratulations; a folded lower left corner meant good-bye; and a folded lower right corner signified condolences.

A married woman had two cards—one with her own name and one with her husband's name. She would leave her husband's card even when he wasn't with her. She always used her husband's full name, but her daughters' cards read "Miss Jones" or "The Misses Jones," as if they didn't have first names!

Foreword

A lady didn't have her address printed on her card, since this implied that she was begging for visitors. Business cards were popular but no polite person would ever present a business card on a social visit.

"At home" manners. In higher social circles, people often set aside one day each week when they were "at home" to friends who cared to visit. In large cities, whole neighborhoods might open their doors on the same day. On these special days, the entry and parlor would be spotless and the hosts dressed in their best attire. Tea and cakes or sandwiches were served, and conversation was supposed to be light and cheerful.

Many Victorian rules of visiting still apply today: Don't take pets, young children, or people unknown to the host unless they were invited. Dress appropriately. Don't lounge on the furniture. Don't play music unless asked to by the host. Don't say anything that might cause offense. Leave before the visit becomes tiresome.

Throughout a formal visit, Victorian ladies kept their capes and bonnets on, and men held their hats. All guests wore or held their gloves. Men were warned against warming their backs at the fireplace; sitting with crossed legs was considered uncouth. A gentleman never sat next to a woman unless she requested.

The rules of calling were more strictly followed in cities and large towns than in country communities and on the frontier. Most hardworking Americans didn't have the time for formal visiting and couldn't afford servants to greet callers. People in rural areas often lived at some distance from their neighbors, so visits were less frequent and more casual.

ix

∾ THE LANGUAGE OF FLOWERS ∾

Victorians used flowers as symbols of thoughts and feelings that well-bred men and women were not supposed to express in polite company. A young man who had slighted or behaved rudely to a girl he liked might make amends by sending her a bouquet including brambles for remorse, snowdrops for hope, and periwinkles for friendship. By reading the code of the flowers, the girl would know that he regretted his behavior and hoped to continue the friendship.

Different varieties of flowers carried different and sometimes contradictory meanings. For example, a red rose meant "I love you" but deep red roses indicated shame. Red and white roses combined meant unity and might be mixed in a bride's bouquet.

Queen Victoria included myrtle, the symbol of love and affection, in her wedding bouquet. At her wish, the myrtle was planted, and British royal brides traditionally include a bit of Queen Victoria's myrtle in their bouquets or wedding decorations.

In times of grief, sympathy might be expressed with marigolds (sorrow) or geraniums (comfort). Zinnias from absent friends meant they were thinking of the recipient. Pansies spoke of thoughtfulness, daffodils of regard, and dogwood of durability.

The language of flowers could also be negative. The fragrant lavender indicated distrust, the prickly thistle signaled defiance, the sunflower symbolized haughtiness, basil meant hate, and the wild yarrow was a declaration of war.

Foreword

∞ ATTENTION DANCES AND BALLS ∞

In the 1800s, dances were very popular, but when the number of guests swelled beyond fifty people, the dance officially became a ball. Grand Victorian houses included ballrooms large enough to accommodate several hundred dancers, and people in "high society" often hosted elaborate balls, and a family's social reputation could hinge on whether they received invitations to these exclusive events.

For most people, however, dances were a Saturday night occasion, usually starting at sundown after the week's work was completed. Public dances might also be held after another event, such as a concert. A dance usually began with the Grand March — a parade of dancers around the dance floor, led by the highest ranking military or political official and his dance partner. The dances that followed were divided into *sets*, or sessions of dances between which came intermissions.

Rich and poor alike enjoyed rousing traditional and folk dances such as the Virginia reel and the *contredanse* (French for "country dance"). In a land of immigrants, new dances like the polka were introduced. Various forms of the *quadrille* — a square dance for four couples — and circle and line dancing were especially popular. The waltz, a couple's dance in which the man holds the woman's waist, scandalized many people when it was first introduced, but soon became one of the favorite dances.

One of the motives for dances and balls was to bring eligible young people together, so dancers were expected to change their partners throughout the evening. To set the tone, husbands and wives were discouraged from dancing together after the Grand March.

The etiquette of Victorian dances and balls was much more rigid than today's party manners. The dancing itself could be quite energetic and fun, but proper Victorians had to obey rules of conduct like these:

• A lady never entered or crossed a ballroom by herself or asked a man for a dance. A woman never left the room alone.

• At private dances, it was the host's duty to see that every woman danced and, if necessary, to prod male guests to do the right thing.

• A man requested a dance by saying something like "Will you honor me with your hand for the next set?"

• A lady tried never to refuse a request to dance unless she was committed to dance with someone else.

• Everyone wore white gloves and removed them only to eat.

• Women could talk politely, though not too much, to their dance partners. Except for a polite thank you, women weren't expected to continue conversation once the dance was over.

There were people who disapproved of dancing for a variety of reasons including religious scruples. So it was polite for hostesses and hosts not to invite anyone who was opposed to dancing. Good hosts also considered the abilities of their guests — leaving out those whose dancing skills were limited or nonexistent.

TRAVILLA/DINSMORE FAMILY TREE

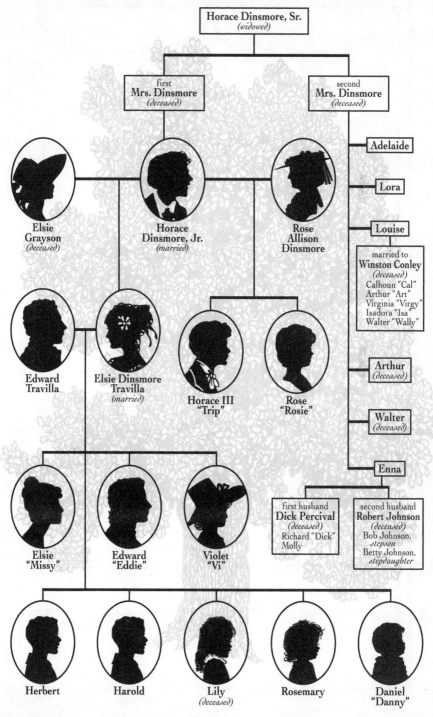

SETTING

The story opens at Ion plantation in mid-April of 1879.

CHARACTERS

∞ ION ∞

Elsie Dinsmore Travilla, Violet's mother and the recently widowed daughter of Horace Dinsmore, Jr., and her children:

> **Elsie ("Missy"),** age 21. Missy is engaged to **Lester Leland**, an artist studying in Rome, Italy.
>
> **Edward ("Ed"),** age 20, a university student.
>
> **Violet ("Vi"),** age 15
>
> **Herbert and Harold,** the twins, age 13
>
> **Rosemary,** age 8
>
> **Daniel ("Danny"),** age 4 1/2

Aunt Chloe—Elsie's faithful maid and companion, and **Joe**, her elderly husband.

Ben—chief servant at Ion, and his wife, **Crystal**, the head housekeeper.

∞ THE OAKS ∞

Horace Dinsmore, Jr.—Violet's grandfather, owner of The Oaks plantation.

Rose Allison Dinsmore—his second wife and mother of **Horace ("Trip") Dinsmore, III**, and **Rosie Dinsmore**; Violet's step-grandmother.

∞ ROSELANDS ∞

Horace Dinsmore, Sr. — Violet's great-grandfather, a widower, owner of Roselands plantation.

Louise Dinsmore Conley — widowed daughter of Horace, Sr., and mother of three grown sons (**Cal, Arthur, Walter**) and two daughters, **Virginia**, age 25, and **Isa**, age 23.

∞ LANSDALE, OHIO ∞

Aunt Wealthy Stanhope — Horace Dinsmore, Jr.'s elderly aunt.

Phyllis Gleeson and her adult son, **Simon** — devoted employees of Aunt Wealthy.

Richard and Lottie Allison — Rose Dinsmore's brother and his wife; also long-time friends of Elsie Travilla. Their daughter, **Katie**, is 13.

Reverend and Mrs. Swift and their daughter, **Constance.**

Mr. and Mrs. Montgomery — a farming couple, and their four sons and one daughter, **Abby.**

Marcia and **Stuart Keith**, **Millie Keith Landreth**, and other members of Aunt Wealthy's family.

∞ OTHERS ∞

Harry Duncan — Wealthy's nephew who is married to Rose Dinsmore's youngest sister, May.

Mrs. Maureen O'Flaherty — housekeeper of Viamede, the Travilla plantation in Louisiana.

James Keith — the minister at Viamede and a cousin of the Dinsmores and the Travillas.

Mr. Mitchell Love—an old friend of Horace Dinsmore, Jr.; Mr. Love and his daughter, **Zoe**, 14, live in Italy.

Dr. Di Marco—a physician.

Mrs. Warden—an English nurse.

Mrs. Constanza—a widow with two young children, **Alberto** and **Angelina**.

CHAPTER

1

A Letter from Ohio

*"If you consider me a believer in
the Lord," she said, "come
and stay at my house."
And she persuaded us.*

ACTS 16:15

It was an unnaturally warm and clear afternoon for mid-April. The bright sun—now dipping toward the west—transformed the line of tall trees on the opposite side of the lake. The tender green leaves glowed with suffused sunlight, and even the smallest branches seemed to be etched in high relief. It appeared as if nature had made a chapel of the place and decorated it with stained glass windows that were beyond the creative abilities of any human artist.

A girl sat at the end of the low wooden dock that projected into the lake. She had tossed aside her jacket and bonnet, removed her shoes and stockings, and gathered her skirts up above her knees so that she seemed to be sitting in a puff of pink. Her legs dangled over the edge of the dock, and she was lazily scissoring her feet back and forth in the water, creating ripples that caught the light as they expanded outward in coppery circles.

Having come upon this idyllic vision, Horace Dinsmore approached quietly—the new grass muting his footsteps. Something in him did not want to disturb the picture. The slim and dark-haired girl, the water, the light through the trees—these were the elements of a painting in the new style, and though there was no artist available to catch the scene on canvas, Horace wanted to capture it in his mind and hold it there.

But he reached the dock, and the sound of his boots on its thick planks broke the spell. Without changing her position, the girl turned her head and looked back over her shoulder. Seeing her grandfather, she waved and started to rise, but Horace stopped her.

3

"Stay where you are, Vi dear," he said, "and I will join you."

He took his seat on a camp stool that he found there along with several pads of paper and an open box of pastel colors. A sheet of paper was pinned to a board, and Horace saw an unfinished drawing of the living landscape before him.

"You've abandoned your sketch?" he inquired.

Violet gazed out over the lake. "It's so hard to get the color right," she said. "I thought that if I stopped struggling and just looked at what is in front of me. . . well, inspiration might strike."

"Is the water cold?"

"Yes, sir, but not uncomfortably so."

They fell silent, and for some minutes they both looked across the lake, listened to its gentle lapping, and basked in the peacefulness around them.

"I did have a purpose in seeking you out, my dear," Horace said at last. "I've come with an invitation."

She looked up quizzically. "For me?" she asked.

Horace reached into his coat pocket and pulled forth a thick sheaf of notepapers. "I received this today from Aunt Wealthy Stanhope, and here amid all the news of Lansdale and our Northern friends and relatives, she has extended an invitation to you to visit her."

"I don't understand, Grandpapa," Vi said. "Are we not going to Ohio in June, for her birthday and the family reunion?"

"We are, but she has written that she would like you to come early and stay with her for the month prior. I think she is anxious to meet you, for you have much in common, including your June birthdays. Wealthy invited Missy, too, but I think my eldest granddaughter does not want to spend an additional month away from home."

"She might miss a letter from her Lester," Vi laughed.

"True," Horace said, "but I believe her reasoning is somewhat more substantial. Now that Lester's return is set for the fall and their wedding planned for next December, Missy will give up her teaching at the end of May. She doesn't want to leave her pupils early. Your sister has been of great service to Mr. Gaylord at the school this year."

Vi knew very well how dedicated Missy was to the work she was doing as assistant to the new master of the plantation school. "She's like you, Grandpapa. A natural teacher."

"At any rate, she has decided to decline Wealthy's invitation and wait to accompany the rest of us in June," Horace said. "But what do you think of spending a month with your great-great-aunt?"

Vi needed only a few moments to reflect. "I want to go, Grandpapa. I'm terribly curious about Aunt Wealthy and Lansdale, and I should like to be there to help her if I can."

"She doesn't say so in her letter," Horace said, passing the pages to Vi, "but I think she can use some assistance. Lottie and Richard Allison are handling all the planning and organizing of the reunion, but I'm sure Aunt Wealthy is involved. And I know that you will enjoy her, for though her age is almost a hundred, her mind and spirit are as youthful as ever. She's also quite an artist in her way."

This last comment surprised Vi. "Does she paint?" the girl asked.

"No, her artistry is more a matter of style," Horace replied with a smile. "As you will see from the moment you first set eyes on her, Aunt Wealthy is an individualist."

"I've heard about her odd dress, and her letters are those of one who does not exactly conform to what is expected," Vi said.

"Little of what Aunt Wealthy does is expected," Horace went on, "and yet she never violates a rule of etiquette nor a standard of hospitality and graciousness. She lives her faith in everything she does. Her letters only hint at the conversations you will enjoy, for Wealthy is very intelligent and has a gift for seeing things in unconventional ways. I believe that you will find her a kindred spirit to yourself, my girl, and a most delightful hostess."

"Do you think that I'm unconventional, Grandpapa?" Vi asked as she rose and began to gather her things.

"I think you are," Horace responded honestly. "And I think that your unconventionality is a virtue to be cultivated." He stood and folded the little stool. "We are entering a new age, Vi. When my father was a boy, most of the people in this country were farmers or artisans who worked with their hands. Now we are becoming a nation of great cities and industries. In many ways, our nation is being reborn, and the challenges are unlike any we have faced before. We will need unconventional thinkers like you, my girl, who are not fearful of change."

Vi looked closely into his face and saw that he was not teasing her. "You mean that," she said.

"I do," he replied. He laid a strong hand on her shoulder and added, "I want you never to be afraid of your individuality, Vi, for it is one of God's many gifts to you. I'm glad that you will have this visit with Wealthy. There is much about her to comfort and perhaps inspire you."

Vi, who could hardly imagine herself being of much significance to the changing nation her grandfather had spoken of, smiled and said, "Do you mind if I challenge convention by walking home barefooted, Grandpapa? It's not very lady-like, but I love the feel of the grass between my toes."

Horace clapped a hand on her back. "I'd be disappointed if you didn't," he laughed. "I've half a mind to shake off my boots and do the same."

Her big, dark eyes grew even bigger. "And will you?" she asked.

"Only *half* a mind," he said as they turned toward Ion.

"Then perhaps you should remove only one boot," Vi laughed. "That would violate only half a convention."

Vi restored her shoes to her feet before they reached the house, and so she was acceptably shod when she and her grandfather entered her mother's sitting room. Elsie and Rose Dinsmore were there, a tea tray on a low table between them.

Vi went first to kiss her mother, then her grandmother. She eagerly accepted the cup of tea Rose offered her and settled into a nearby chair.

"Did you bring back a picture for us?" Elsie asked.

"Not today, Mamma," Vi said. "I'm having trouble with the light and how it affects the color of everything. I am afraid that it is beyond my skills. I do think that spring is the most difficult season to paint. But I will keep working at getting it right."

"So you aren't disappointed?"

"Oh, no, Mamma," Vi answered firmly. "Besides, I got to talk with Grandpapa and received an invitation from Aunt Wealthy." She reached for a sandwich and said, "It was a productive afternoon, though I didn't complete my drawing."

"And how will you reply to Wealthy's invitation?" Rose asked.

"I will accept with pleasure," Vi smiled happily.

"And pleasure is just what you shall receive," Elsie said. "My own first visit with Aunt Wealthy was one of the most memorable times of my girlhood. I had simply never encountered anyone like my great-aunt," Elsie continued. "Nor Lottie and Nellie King and their dear parents. And the Nickles."

Horace burst into a laugh. "The Nickles!" he exclaimed as the memory of the family who ran the boarding house across the street from Wealthy Stanhope flooded back. "What was the little girl's name? She was a delightfully impish child."

"It was Willy, Papa," Elsie said. "Lenwilla Ellawea Nickle and her brother, Corbinus. I believe their widowed mother eventually married and the family moved to California."

"Lansdale itself is much altered since that time," Horace said. "It is a true city now, not the quaint little town we visited thirty years ago."

Vi contented herself with several more sandwiches and another cup of tea as she listened to her mother and grandparents reminisce about Ohio and Aunt Wealthy and the Stanhope and Keith families. It was when her grandfather mentioned something about the circuitous train trip that he and Elsie had taken to Lansdale that Vi spoke up.

"How will I get to Lansdale?" she asked.

"Ah, I've been considering that," her mother said. "The train route is more direct now, and the journey is several days shorter. We can send your trunks in advance, Vi, so you need not have that worry."

"Am I to travel alone?" Vi asked in astonishment.

"Hardly," Horace replied instantly.

"Though I would trust you on such a trip," Elsie said, "it would not be proper for a girl your age."

"Or even Missy's age," Horace added firmly.

Elsie smiled ever so slightly. For all his modern ideas, her father was still a true believer in the chivalry of the Old South, at least as far as the protection of women was concerned.

"Neither I nor your grandparents can make the trip, for we have business here that must be attended to before June," Elsie continued. "But I have a solution that you may find acceptable, Vi. Cousin James has written me from Viamede, and he reports that Aunt Mamie is almost completely well now. This means that Mrs. O'Flaherty may be able to take time from her duties to be your traveling companion. Would that be agreeable to you?"

At the mention of the name of Viamede's Irish housekeeper, a broad smile came to Vi's face. "Oh, that would be perfect!" she declared.

"Then I'll write to her immediately," Elsie said. "If she agrees and Viamede can spare her for six weeks, she can come here to Ion, and the two of you will depart for Lansdale in the first week of May."

Envisioning herself and the fascinating Mrs. O'Flaherty embarking together for Ohio somehow made the trip become real for Vi. *How exciting! This is the best birthday present I could ever hope for.*

Violet's Amazing Summer

"When did you last see Aunt Wealthy?" Missy asked her mother later that night. Elsie and her older daughters were in Vi's bedroom and had just completed their Bible reading.

"She came to our wedding," Elsie recalled, "and your father and I were most flattered. Her nephew Harry Duncan came with her, and it was on that occasion that he first met your cousin May."

"How romantic," Missy sighed, for romance was much on her mind with her fiancé's return from Italy and their wedding now less than nine months away.

"Not really, for May was quite young," Elsie said. "Their romance did not blossom until she and Harry met again during the war. But now that I think of it, several matches were previewed at our wedding. That was also the first time your Uncle Richard Allison laid eyes on my dear friend Lottie King."

"I can't wait to see Mrs. Allison again," Vi said. "I remember when they visited Grandpapa and Grandmamma a few years ago, but I didn't realize then how interesting Mrs. Allison is. To think—a college graduate. She is a real pioneer."

"Indeed, she is," Elsie smiled. She leaned forward and placed her hand on Vi's, squeezing it warmly. "You are going to meet many good people. Lottie and Richard have a daughter, you know, who is nearly the same age as Harold and Herbert."

"Will the Duncans come to the reunion?" Missy asked. "It's been a long time since we saw Aunt May and Uncle Harry and their children."

"I'm sure they will be there," Elsie replied. "Chicago is not so far from Lansdale, and Harry would not miss Wealthy's birthday for the world."

"We do have a big family," Vi said. "I shall have to make a list of their names if I am to remember everyone."

"God has truly blessed us with a wealth of family," Elsie agreed. "Do you remember the apostle Paul's teaching about widows? 'But if a widow has children or grandchildren, these should learn first of all to put their religion into practice by caring for their own family and so repaying their parents and grandparents, for this is pleasing to God.'

"I believe this is a message for all, that caring for our families is pleasing to our Lord. That's why I'm so happy about the forthcoming reunion in Lansdale. There have been rifts in our family, but they are now healed, and this gathering will at last bring us together again. Indeed, there will be many new names to learn. Perhaps, Vi dearest, you can make your list during your time with Aunt Wealthy, for she has the longest memory of the family."

Vi thought this a good idea and resolved to commit her family list to her journal. That thought brought another.

"Will Molly and Mr. Embury attend the reunion?" she asked.

"No," Elsie said. "They are very busy preparing for their new baby. In any case, Molly is not related to Aunt Wealthy, and this reunion is for family of the Stanhope line. If we were to gather the members of all our family, I am afraid the city of Lansdale would burst at its seams."

"Then might we visit Viamede again soon, Mamma?" Missy asked. "I miss Molly so very much."

"Perhaps we can," Elsie said. "I had not planned for us to travel this summer, after our Lansdale visit. But we all might benefit from a trip to Viamede, though it will be hot there in the summer."

"It will be hot here, too," Vi said matter-of-factly.

"Well, that's true," her mother agreed. "I will think about it. Now, however, it is late. Missy, will you begin our prayer?"

Prayers were said, kisses exchanged, and Elsie and Missy soon retired to their rooms. Vi extinguished her light and settled under her covers. But sleep did not come easily. Her mind almost bubbled with anticipation — the journey to Ohio, seeing Mrs. O'Flaherty again, meeting Aunt Wealthy and so many new people. And now, the possibility of a return to Viamede…. She hugged her pillow and smiled at the dark. *It's going to be a wonderful summer*, she thought happily. *I just know that it's going to be the most amazingly exciting summer I've ever had.*

2

A Red-Carpet Welcome

Share with God's people who are in need. Practice hospitality.

ROMANS 12:13

A Red-Carpet Welcome

*T*he train pulled slowly into Lansdale with a great grinding of brakes and hooting of its whistle. Though it was a fine, clear morning, Vi's first views of the city were all but obscured by the white clouds of steam that billowed from the train.

"Who will meet us, do you think?" she asked as she peered out the dusty window at the thick veil of steam and smoke.

"I know only one way to find out," said Mrs. O'Flaherty. She was checking the luggage rack to be sure that nothing was left behind. "Come away from that window now, and let's be gone. Have you got your purse? And your book? Good. Now check your hat in that mirror. It's a bit at a tilt. There. You look perfect."

Her hat in place, Vi hurried from the train compartment and followed Mrs. O'Flaherty into the narrow corridor. Their luggage was stacked near the exit, and a porter waited to assist passengers down the metal steps onto the platform. Vi's foot had hardly touched ground when she heard her name called out. Looking up, she saw a woman of her mother's age and a girl of about thirteen.

"Violet!" the woman called, and rushed toward her. "My goodness, how you have grown. Do you remember me? I'm Lottie Allison, and this is my daughter, Katherine. And we are your welcoming party."

There followed a quick embrace, after which Vi introduced Mrs. O'Flaherty to the Allisons. With the brisk precision of a military commander, Mrs. Allison directed another porter to gather the bags and take them to a waiting carriage.

"Your Uncle Richard asked me to convey his apologies for being unable to meet you, but you'll see him this evening," Mrs. Allison said as the four women walked down the platform toward the station itself.

The noise was so great that further conversation was impossible until they had exited the station — a large building that was obviously still under construction — and reached the street. Mrs. Allison led them to an open carriage, saw that the baggage was quickly stowed, and generously tipped both the porter and the young man who was tending the horses. He handed Mrs. O'Flaherty, Vi, and Katherine into their seats. Then, to Vi's great surprise, Mrs. Allison climbed onto the driver's seat, took the reins, and expertly guided the vehicle into the road.

"I would give you the grand tour," said Mrs. Allison, "but I have been admonished by your Aunt Wealthy to take the most direct route to her house."

Then Katherine spoke up for the first time. "The last thing Wealthy said to us was 'no time for *seesighting*,' " she giggled.

"You call her Wealthy?" Vi asked.

"She insists," Katherine said. "I know it sounds impertinent, and I always address her as Miss Stanhope when we're in company. But among family and good friends, which you and Mrs. O'Flaherty are, she positively refuses to answer to anything but Wealthy or Aunt Wealthy. Oh, and my mother is really hoping that you will call her Aunt Lottie. And I'm Katherine Charlotte, but I wish you'd call me Katie."

The area around the station was clearly the business section of Lansdale, and Vi saw an impressive number of shops and office buildings. But she had little opportunity to register any specifics, for Lottie was urging the horses forward at a fast trot. Soon, small houses began to replace commercial buildings, and then they turned onto a wide, tree-lined boulevard where the homes were of grander scale with expansive, well-groomed lawns and formal gardens.

After several blocks, Lottie slowed the pace, and Katie pointed out a handsome brick house — two stories with an elegant columned entrance and what appeared to be a domed top.

"That's our house," Katie said. "You'll see it tonight when you come for supper."

Vi wanted to know more, but just past the Allisons' house, the carriage turned again, and they entered a much narrower street where the houses were older and plainer in style.

"Can you guess which is Wealthy's?" Katie smiled.

Vi peered from side to side, and then she, too, smiled.

The carriage came to a halt before a gabled brick house trimmed in pristine white and with a wide porch crossing its entire front. A fence of iron rails enclosed the yard, but its gate stood open, and Vi could see that a bright scarlet strip ran straight up the path and the porch steps to the front door.

"Wealthy doesn't roll out her red carpet for any but the most special guests," Lottie said as she drew the carriage to a halt.

A man came rushing from the house. Lottie intoduced him as Simon Gleeson.

"How do you do, Mr. Gleeson?" Vi said.

"Just fine, Miss Violet. Now if you ladies will let me help you down, there's someone waiting for you inside, and she's about to bust with excitement."

Simon gave his hand to Vi, then Mrs. O'Flaherty.

"You coming, Miss Katie?" he asked.

"We're going home, Simon," Lottie replied before her daughter could speak, "to stable the horse and wash off the dust. We'll return at noon for lunch." Then she added in a confidential tone, "I'm allowing Katie to play truant today, since this is a very special occasion."

Simon grinned up at Katie. "And here I was thinking that you talked your way out of a school day."

He turned to the guests. "Miss Violet and Mrs. O'Flaherty, please go on in, and I'll bring these bags. Your trunks are here, and your rooms are ready."

So Vi and Mrs. O'Flaherty walked quickly up the red carpet. They were met at the door by a woman who introduced herself as the housekeeper, and ignoring further courtesies, she bustled them toward the living room.

A tiny woman sat in an armchair that seemed almost to swallow her in its bright chintz upholstery. But there was no chintz in the world that could distract from Aunt Wealthy. She sat erect, her diminutive size heightened by a tight bun of white hair that rose at least four inches above the top of her head. Wire-rimmed spectacles perched low upon her nose and seemed to outline her pink cheeks. She was dressed in a simple gown of dark green with a white lace collar, but a fringed shawl of creamy silk embroidered with brilliant red poppies was draped around her shoulders and pinned at one side with a large silver butterfly that seemed to perch just below her ear. Vi's immediate impression was of a model posed in a setting designed to challenge an artist's mastery of color and texture.

At the sight of her great-great-niece, Aunt Wealthy's face came wonderfully alive. Her smile was wide and warm. (Vi would later learn that among her aunt's very few vanities were her teeth, which were all her own.)

"Come here, Vi," the little lady said in a voice of surprising strength and clarity.

Vi swiftly complied, approaching and bending to kiss her aunt's cheek. The old lady took the girl's hand and bid her to sit on the little ottoman beside the chair.

Behind her wire-rimmed spectacles, Aunt Wealthy's eyes glittered.

"It's so good to be here," Vi said. "I cannot tell you how much I have looked forward to meeting you, Aunt Wealthy."

"Oh, my child, this is a day that the Lord has truly blessed."

Aunt Wealthy held on to Vi's hand and like a bird, cocked her head to the left, then the right. "So like," she said softly. "So very like."

Vi did not understand what her aunt meant until Wealthy said, "I see much of your beautiful mother in you, my dear, but your resemblance to your father is remarkable, and Mr. Vanilla was quite the handsomest man I ever saw. Your eyes and the set of your chin and the dark of your hair—to see your lovely face brings back memories that gladden my old heart."

"Thank you, Aunt Wealthy," Vi said, smiling at the compliment and her aunt's confusion of her father's name.

"Ah, I see you also inherited his dimple."

"That is what people say, though I don't notice it."

"Well, it's hard to see ourselves smile, isn't it? My guess is that you are not the type of girl who wastes much time at mirrors."

Wealthy leaned slightly forward and in a lowered tone said, "I have not met your friend."

Vi instantly recalled herself. "Mrs. O'Flaherty, please come meet my Aunt Wealthy Stanhope."

It was now Mrs. O'Flaherty's turn to approach. "It is a pleasure to meet you, Miss Stanhope," she said.

Wealthy looked up at the tall woman and actually grinned. "Thank you for accompanying my niece on her journey, Mrs. O'Flaherty. Do I hear Ireland in your voice?"

"You do, ma'am, for I am a native of the Isles."

"Then we shall have some interesting talks, I hope. These days I rarely travel in body. But I often set my mind on the road, and your country is one I would dearly like to visit."

Mrs. O'Flaherty smiled, displaying her gold tooth, and said, "I believe that I can escort you there, Miss Stanhope, if you are not averse to flying upon the wings of imagination."

Wealthy, who had not relinquished her hold on Vi, extended her other hand to Mrs. O'Flaherty and said, "I am so pleased to welcome you to my home. Most pleased. But now I think that you and Vi will want to see your rooms and perhaps rest a bit before lunch. Phyllis will show you the way. Lottie and young Katie will be here for luncheon, and I hope you will join us, Mrs. O'Flaherty."

"Most gladly," Mrs. O'Flaherty said.

"I've never had a red carpet spread out for me," Vi said. "It is a most delightful welcome, Aunt Wealthy."

"It had noble beginnings, dear," Wealthy responded. "I once had a neighbor, a widow named Mrs. Penny—or was it Nickle? A charming but somewhat peculiar woman. She made that rug from scrap cloth and dye, and presented it to me one Christmas before she moved away. I was never sure what she expected me to do with it, but it makes a cheerful statement, don't you think?"

The housekeeper suddenly appeared at Wealthy's side and motioned for Vi and Mrs. O'Flaherty to follow her. Wealthy gave Vi's hand a last pat. "Phyllis has untrunked your pack and dressed your wardrobe, dear," she said, "so you will not be wrinkled."

Once in the pretty upstairs bedroom that was to be hers, Vi thanked Phyllis for unpacking her trunk and hanging her dresses in the wardrobe. Phyllis laughed heartily: "Sometimes Miss Wealthy speaks in strange tongues, but you took her meaning quick enough. I remember that your mother required several days to catch on the first time she came to visit us."

"You were here then?" Vi asked.

"I've been with Miss Wealthy for nigh on thirty years, Miss Vi. Since my husband passed away and Miss Wealthy asked me and my boy Simon to move in with her."

"Then you are Mrs. Gleeson," Vi said, putting two and two together.

"I am," the housekeeper said, "but I'd be pleased if you call me Phyllis. I know it's not what's exactly proper, but we tend to go by first names when it's just us. Miss Wealthy's never been much for rules that set people apart."

"In that way, she's like my Papa," Vi remarked.

"Oh, your Papa," Phyllis said, smiling wistfully. "He and Miss Wealthy always got on like a house afire. She said he was the smartest and kindest man that ever stepped across the doorstep, as well as the best looking."

Phyllis's expression changed as she continued, "We were all mighty sorry to hear about your father, Miss Vi."

"Thank you," Vi said simply.

"Now you relax yourself while I see that Mrs. O'Flaherty is settled in. I imagine Miss Wealthy will be napping in her chair till lunch. She gets tired out nowadays. If you'd like to freshen up, the bathroom's down at the far end of the hallway. It's practically brand new and Miss Wealthy's pride and joy.

You'd think a woman her age would be slow to change her ways. But not Miss Wealthy. We have bathrooms upstairs and down and steam heat and a clothes washer."

At that, Phyllis went to the door but paused briefly before leaving. "This was your mother's room when she stayed with us, Miss Vi, and not much is changed except for the addition of that steam radiator. I hope you like it. If you or Mrs. O'Flaherty should want some company, come on down to the kitchen. I've got hot tea and cold lemonade."

Vi looked around her room. It was not even half the size of her bedroom at Ion, and most of its area was taken up by a large brass bed and a tall wardrobe. There was also a small desk and chair, a dresser, and a bedside table. The room was located at the front of the house, and its two windows overlooked the garden and the street.

There was little of luxury about the room, but a great deal of charm. The walls were papered in a pattern of pale pink and yellow roses, and the bed linens were white. A Persian carpet of intricate design covered the floor.

Despite the simplicity of the room, its décor spoke of a finely developed eye for beauty. On the desk, pink peonies cascaded from a sapphire blue vase of blown glass that Vi guessed was Venetian. The bedside table was draped in an old but still beautiful silk Spanish shawl like the one that Aunt Wealthy wore. And above the bed hung a small framed painting that Vi immediately recognized as an excellent example of the Hudson River school.

She sat down on the bed and contemplated her first hour in Lansdale. Odd, she thought, that she already felt so completely at home here. *Did I really just meet Aunt Wealthy?* she asked herself. *I feel as if I have always known her.*

Vi looked about her again. *I wonder if Mamma felt this way when she stayed in this room? It is very different from home and yet familiar, too. Somehow, I know that I am not a stranger in this house.* A bit of verse from Proverbs came to her: "He blesses the home of the righteous."

A knock at her door interrupted her thoughts, and Mrs. O'Flaherty entered. "Do you have everything you need?" she asked.

Vi smiled and replied, "Oh, yes. Everything. And how is your room?"

Mrs. O'Flaherty glanced quickly around, then said, "Like a twin to this one, save that my walls are dressed in blue, and the painting above my bed is a still life of fruits and flowers. Phyllis wanted me to tell you that there are plenty of towels in the bathroom."

Vi's mind was not on towels. "You traveled a longer way than I to get here, Mrs. O'Flaherty. Are you glad you came?"

A smile played on Mrs. O'Flaherty's face. "I have traveled much longer and farther than you know, my girl, and I have learned to trust my sense of place. I know nothing of Lansdale save what we saw from the carriage, but I seem to know this house. I believe that a house takes its spirit from its people, and this house beckons the stranger in and bids her welcome. Yes, I am very glad to be here. And you?"

"Oh, you said just what I have been thinking," Vi replied happily.

Luncheon was spent almost exclusively in conversation about the Travillas and the Dinsmores, for Aunt Wealthy and Lottie were eager to hear all the news of their Southern family and friends.

"I fear we will tire you out, Vi dear," Lottie Allison said at last, "with all our questions. It is just that even your mother's fascinating letters are no substitute for an eye-witness account."

"I don't mind at all, Aunt Lottie," Vi replied truthfully, her use of the familiar name winning a sweet smile of pleasure from Mrs. Allison.

"Well, you may now turn the tables on us, dear girl," Wealthy said. "What would you like to know about Lansdale?"

"I hardly know where to begin," Vi said. "Lansdale is a much larger town than I expected, although Grandpapa said it has grown since his first visit."

"Oh, you must say *city*," Aunt Wealthy declared. "Our mayor, whom you will meet on Sunday, is quite insistent that we are now a *real city*. Those of us who have been here longer than he still think of Lansdale as a small town," she added with a wry smile, "but I suppose our mayor is correct."

"It was still a country town when Richard and I married and moved here after the war," Mrs. Allison added. "We had planned only to visit and then return to Philadelphia. But my darling husband fell in love with Lansdale at first sight. To me, it was home, but Richard saw opportunity. Lansdale brought out his pioneer spirit."

"Have you ever met my Papa?" Katie asked Vi.

"Once, when your parents visited my grandparents," Vi said, "but I was too young to remember him well."

24

"You'll like him," Katie said with the assurance of a daughter who can imagine no father as good and kind as her own.

"And you will meet him again tonight, when you and Wealthy dine with us," Lottie added.

"Tonight we will be *en famille*, as the French say," Wealthy explained. "Just Lottie, Richard, our Katie, and Lottie's father, Dr. King."

"And we would be most pleased if you will join us, Mrs. O'Flaherty," Lottie said.

A few minutes later, Phyllis quietly entered the dining room. Catching sight of her, Wealthy said to her guests, "We seem to be finished. Perhaps we might sit on the porch a while."

As Vi watched, both the Allisons rose and went to Wealthy, and with gentle, practiced care, they helped her from her chair. Leaning on Lottie's arm, Wealthy stood still for several moments and then began to make her way slowly but steadily across the dining room, through the living room, and toward the front door. Katie waltzed ahead to hold the screened door wide for Wealthy and her mother.

Vi was following when Katie called, "Will you bring that little basket beside the couch?"

Vi looked around, saw the basket on a low table, and took it up. When she got to the door, Katie said, "That's Aunt Wealthy's knitting. She's making a shawl for one of the elderly ladies who attends our church." Lowering her voice to a whisper, she added, "Aunt Wealthy is always doing something kind for someone."

"And I can see that you and your mother are very kind to her," Vi said in a soft tone that matched Katie's.

The younger girl looked surprised. "Are we? Goodness, I don't think of it that way. Aunt Wealthy does so much for us that it's just normal to do for her, isn't it?"

Vi smiled. "I suppose it is," she said. Then an idea struck her, and she said, "I really want to be of assistance to my aunt while I'm here. Will you help me, Katie? Will you tell me what I can do for her?"

Katie's own smile broadened. "Oh, I should be glad to," she said gaily. Vi's request pleased her greatly, for it was the type of thing one asked of a friend.

"But where is Mrs. O'Flaherty?" Wealthy asked as Vi handed her the basket and then took her seat beside Katie on the porch swing.

"She wanted to help Phyllis," Vi explained. "I can get her if you like."

"No, dear, that's alright. Phyllis will enjoy her company," Wealthy said. "Now, tell me what you would like to do this afternoon."

"Whatever you suggest, Aunt Wealthy," Vi replied.

"Then I suggest that Katie show you the house and garden. The sooner you are comfortable, the better. I want you and Mrs. O'Flaherty to come and go as you like. We are somewhat more casual in our style here in Ohio than you may be used to."

Vi said, "I would like a tour, if Katie has the time." To which Katie nodded energetically.

"We've planned some activities for the next few days," Wealthy went on. "Nothing elaborate, but I want you to meet my neighbors. I do believe I have the best neighbors in the world." Laying her hand on Lottie's, she added, "I could not get along without them."

"Oh, Aunt Wealthy, you need not entertain me," Vi said, for she suddenly became concerned that her visit might be more of a strain than her aunt needed.

"You can't talk her out of it," Lottie laughed. "You might say that we are entertaining you before the storm. The great reunion is just a month away, and everyone is helping. We intend to put you to work too."

"I want to do whatever I can," Vi said with enthusiasm.

"Good," Mrs. Allison said. "But you need not roll up your sleeves quite yet. Tell her what you have scheduled, Aunt Wealthy."

"You already know of our little supper party tonight," the elderly lady said. "Tomorrow, I have invited a number of young ladies to tea. We have some quite remarkable young women here in Lansdale—in addition to our Katie, who has been remarkable since the day of her birth," she said with a warm smile at the girl. "On Friday evening, there is a party at the Fletchers', and knowing that you will meet Amy at tea, I took the liberty of accepting for you," Wealthy continued.

Seeing Vi's confusion, Lottie quickly explained, "Amy Fletcher is one of the young ladies you will meet tomorrow. Her parents are hosting the party on Friday."

"Sunday, we will have Reverend and Mrs. Swift and Mayor Palace and his good wife to dinner after church," Wealthy said.

Lottie laughed, "He is a mere *Castle*, Aunt Wealthy, and not a Palace."

Wealthy laughed as well. "Mayor *Castle* is already quite proud of himself," she said, "and needs no further elevation from me. You must forgive me, Vi dear, for my errors. I might claim that it is the consequence of advanced years, but in fact, I've always tumbled my words. My father said it was the result of a mind that was too quick for words, which is a compassionate but not entirely satisfactory explanation. I have tried to correct myself, but without much success. So I trust my friends to correct me, and you must promise to speak up should I address you as Pansy or Buttercup or some such relation of the delightful violet."

"I promise," Vi replied playfully, "though I would not mind being any flower that comes to mind."

"Oh, Aunt Wealthy," Katie said, "you and Mamma have forgotten about the picnic."

"That's right!" Wealthy said. "Lottie and Richard have arranged an afternoon picnic at their farm on Saturday."

"I didn't know you have a farm, Aunt Lottie," Vi said.

"It's a small place compared to the great plantations of the South," Lottie said. "But there are horses to ride, a pond to fish, and a stream to wade. Now that we have enumerated all the events planned for the next four days, I wonder if we will not exhaust you."

"It all sounds wonderful," Vi protested. "I want to meet your friends and see everything I can of Lansdale."

"Then let's start with your tour," Katie said, planting her feet on the floor to stop the swing's gentle motion.

When Vi and Katie had left, Wealthy spoke softly to Lottie: "Our Vi seems to have not only her father's looks but his inquisitive nature as well."

"I sense that she has more than a drop of Stanhope in her, too," Lottie responded with a gentle smile. "Like you, Aunt Wealthy, she is both openhearted and open-minded. I believe you two are much alike."

CHAPTER 3

Savor the Day

This is the day the LORD has made; let us rejoice and be glad in it.

PSALM 118:24

*T*he first days of Vi's visit were, in fact, almost too full to remember in any detail. Wisely, she determined to use her journal to good effect, and each night before her prayers, she took time to record the day's activities.

The young women of Lansdale whom she met at tea the day after her arrival were, indeed, impressive. Amy Fletcher was a gentle and deeply spiritual young lady of nineteen. Constance Swift, the daughter of the pastor, was a lively and plain-spoken girl about Vi's age. Abigail Montgomery, whose family ran Richard Allison's farm, was a special friend of Katie and very soon won Vi's heart. Abby was an only daughter and the youngest of the five Montgomery children.

At the supper and dance party hosted by Amy Fletcher's family, Vi met more young ladies and quite a few young gentlemen as well, including two of the handsome Montgomery brothers.

Of all the events on the crowded four-day calendar, the picnic at Creekside, the Allisons' farm, stood out most clearly in Vi's mind. The farm was about five miles beyond the outskirts of Lansdale—too great a distance for Aunt Wealthy, who chose to stay at home for the day. It was a working farm primarily devoted to dairy cattle and the production of milk and butter.

On the carriage ride to Creekside, Uncle Richard explained that though he owned the farm, the Montgomerys were purchasing it, and in another few years it would be theirs. "I will miss being a gentleman farmer," he said, "but it's Mr. and Mrs. Montgomery who have turned that land to productive use, and they deserve to own it. I purchased the place not long after Lottie and I moved to Lansdale. It reminded me of my parents' summer home outside Philadelphia."

"My sentimental husband saw the broad fields and the stream at the bottom of the hill, and he was hooked like a trout," Lottie said with a laugh.

Richard laughed too. "I pictured myself wading the stream in rolled-up pants and lying on its mossy banks reading *The Last of the Mohicans*. But I soon discovered that running a farm requires talents I do not possess, and I was lucky enough to find Mr. Montgomery, who had served in the infantry and was recently returned to his wife and children. He is a third-generation farmer in this area and was looking for a place of his own. Our arrangement has proved agreeable to us both for many years now."

On their arrival at Creekside, Vi understood her uncle's attraction to the place. The rambling, two-story farmhouse stood atop a rise and was sheltered by old oak and maple trees. A large barn and silo were not far away. Fences and hedgerows divided the property into large fields; cattle grazed in some areas, but other fields were freshly plowed and ready to be planted with corn or grasses that would be cut for hay. The countryside reminded Vi of Ion, though the Ohio terrain was not so flat.

It was just past noon when the carriage pulled up at the farmhouse. Mr. and Mrs. Montgomery, Abby, and Luke — one of the Montgomery sons whom Vi had met on the previous evening — were waiting on the front porch. When the Allisons, Vi, and Mrs. O'Flaherty had alighted, Luke swung up onto the driver's seat and guided the horses toward the barn. Unnoticed by anyone, he cast a long look back over his shoulder. The object of his attention was, he decided, even prettier in daylight than she had been in the gaslight of the Fletchers' parlor.

"It's a real pleasure to meet you, Miss Travilla and Mrs. O'Flaherty," Mrs. Montgomery declared. "I know that Miss Stanhope must be beside herself to have you for a visit. I've often heard her speak pleasurably of her Southern family. I wish all my boys could be here to meet you, but they're finishing chores and will be along shortly."

"You met Luke and Mark last evening, I believe," Mr. Montgomery said. "Our other 'apostles' are Matthew and John."

"If I'd been a boy, I'd be Peter," Abby giggled. "As it is, I'm Abigail for my mother, who was named after President Adams's wife, and Victoria for the Queen."

Following a snack of cookies and lemonade, hosts and guests divided according to their interests and went in separate directions. Richard and Mr. Montgomery walked to the barn to look over some recently purchased equipment; Lottie and Mrs. O'Flaherty joined Mrs. Montgomery in the kitchen; and Abby took charge of Vi and Katie.

"What would you like to see first?" Abby asked.

"I have heard about the stream," Vi said. "Is it far?"

"Not far, but I'm glad you wore your boots," Abby said.

So off they went, past Mrs. Montgomery's large garden, around the chicken house, and down the hill through a pasture in which colorful wildflowers waved above the new grass. They came to a line of trees, and Vi had the strange feeling that she had gone back in time, for the color of the new leaves was nearly the same as it had been at Ion almost a month earlier.

The creek ran through the wooded area, cutting into the ground to a depth of ten or twelve feet at some points.

Abby led them along a rough path that followed the stream bank, and soon the ground began to slope downward toward the swiftly flowing water. After a bit, the woods seemed to open up, and Vi saw that they had come to a place where flat, smooth, dry boulders rose about a foot above the stream.

"This is my sitting place," Abby said, "when the water is right."

"Isn't it wonderful here?" Katie asked. "I was afraid the water might be too high."

"A week ago, it was," Abby remarked as she sat down on the rock and began to unlace her boots. "It depends on the spring rains. Sometimes this creek is so full it rises right up over its highest banks, and you can hear it roaring all the way up at the house."

Abby and Katie were both soon out of their boots and stockings, and Vi followed their example. When she put her feet in the water, she instantly felt the coldness flow up through her legs.

"I have a place like this at home," she said, wiggling her toes and enjoying the tingling sensation. "It's a small lake, and the water comes from an underground spring so it's always cold. But it doesn't move like this. I like the way this stream tugs at my feet. It's as if it wanted me to run away with it. I wonder where it would take me."

"Well, this creek joins others and spills into the Lansdale River," Abby said, "and that would take you to the Ohio River just below Cincinnati. From there you'd float into the Mississippi and eventually down to the Gulf of Mexico. That's how lots of the settlers got to the South and the West, on river barges. If we lived farther north, the streams would lead you to Lake Erie."

The girls chatted for a while, and Vi learned more about the history of Lansdale.

"My mother says that it was just a pokey little country town when she was a girl, but it's getting to be a real city now, and that's good for the dairy business," Abby said. "City folks need milk and butter, and not many keep their own cows anymore."

"Do you think you're going to like Lansdale, Vi?" asked Katie.

"I already do, especially the people I've met," Vi replied.

"Well, you can't find a better person anywhere than your Aunt Wealthy," Abby declared. "Can you believe that she's going to be a hundred years old? I know she walks kinda slow and all, but she's just as sharp as a needle otherwise. I can't imagine being a hundred years old." She gave a little whistle of amazement.

"Let's see," Vi said. "You're thirteen, right?"

Abby nodded her assent.

"Me, too," Katie added. "We were both born in 1866."

"Then if it is God's will, you will be a hundred in 1966. And I'll be a hundred and three," Vi calculated. "I wonder what the world will be like in 1966. I wonder what people will have invented by then."

That led Vi to mention her summer in Philadelphia during the Centennial of 1876.

"You were really there?" Abby exclaimed. She sat down cross-legged on the rock and riveted her astonished eyes on Vi. "Oh, please tell us what it was like! Did you see the Corliss Engine and Mr. Bell's telephone?"

"Did they really have a big statue made out of butter?" Katie asked; then she added with a skeptical little pout, "And why didn't it melt?"

So for some time Vi both amazed and amused her new young friends with stories of all she had seen at the great Centennial of 1876. Both girls had many questions, and Abby nearly fell over when she heard about the female engineer who ran all the machinery for the Women's Exhibition. "A woman engineer!" she shouted. "I knew it was possible! Just wait till I tell Mark and Luke."

"Will they be surprised?" Vi asked.

"Oh, will they ever," Abby laughed slyly. "As far as my brothers are concerned, we might as well be living in *1766*. They think girls are just good for looking pretty and serving tea and flirting at parties. As if Mamma can't herd cows and guide a plow just as good as any of them. They tease me about my freckles, pull my braid, and call me a tomboy. Do you have brothers, Vi?"

"Four—one is older and away at college, and my baby brother is almost five. But my twin brothers, Harold and Herbert, love to tease. They're your age."

"Twins!" Abby exclaimed. "What if all my brothers had been twins? That would be eight boys to make me crazy!"

Then Abby had another question: "Have you decided what you want to be, Vi, when you grow up?"

"No, but I think about it. Sometimes I want to be a doctor like my cousins Art and Dick. Or an artist like my sister's fiancé. But I had an experience last year that made me think about becoming a missionary."

"But you'd have to go to foreign places to do that," Katie said. "And you'd have to marry a missionary because they wouldn't let a woman go on her own."

"Not really," Vi replied. "I visited a place right here in the United States where people are serving the poor and the sick every day."

"Tell us about it," Abby said.

And Vi did. She told them all about the Carpenters' mission in New Orleans and then about Dinah Carpenter and how she had been a slave, a nursemaid, and a teacher before she and her husband founded the mission. The younger girls listened with wide-eyed attention, and when Vi finished, Abby declared, "That's as exciting as something in a book! Better than most books because the hero is a real woman."

"That makes her a heroine," Katie corrected.

"No difference," Abby sniffed. "She's brave and strong and smart and good. And she serves God by serving others."

Vi smiled and said, "I think there are a great many women like Mrs. Carpenter." She was picturing her own mother, but she continued, "Your mother, Abby, who raised your brothers on her own while your father was at war. And your mother, Katie. She went away to college back when most people thought women's minds were too delicate for advanced study. She taught school, and then she nursed the soldiers throughout the war. I've been told that Aunt Lottie saved many lives with her care."

Abby scrunched her face into a little frown. "I hadn't thought of my Mamma as a hero...heroine. To me, she's just, you know — Mamma."

"Me, too," Katie agreed somewhat solemnly. "My parents are the two people I love most in the world, but I guess that I forget that they are more than my parents. Do you think all children are so self-centered?"

Vi pondered this question for several moments. Then she said, "Yes, I think that's how we all begin. God gives us loving parents to teach us and raise us in His Word. Our mothers and fathers are so much a part of us that we don't think of them as separate from us when we're little. You have four brothers, Abby, and yet do your parents have a favorite?"

Abby grinned, "Well, my brothers say that I'm the pet because I'm the baby and a girl. But truly, I know my parents never set one above the others. I might feel jealous sometimes, but I never feel they love me less because they may give more attention to one of the boys."

"And that's what God wants us to learn from our earthly parents, isn't it?" Vi asked. "He is our Heavenly parent — the Father of us all. If parents can love five children as equally and completely as they love one, isn't that proof that God loves all His children equally?"

Both younger girls looked thoughtful. Then Katie said slowly, "I'd like to serve others by being a teacher. But I'd like to get married and have children, too, and you know they won't let married ladies teach."

"And that's just plain silly," Abby declared. "I'll bet that in 1966 there'll be plenty of lady teachers who're married."

"Mrs. Carpenter has started a school for poor children in the mission in New Orleans," Vi said, "and no one has stopped her."

"I'd like to be President!" Abby proclaimed, puffing out her chest. "Then I'd change all the silly rules about what women can and can't do."

Vi laughed. "If we ever get the right to vote, then I'll vote for you, President Abby," she said.

The girls talked for some time more until a deep male voice rang through the woods: "Food's on!"

"We're coming!" Abby shouted. She reached for her stockings and said, "That's John. He's the quiet one except when he's yelling for me."

"Oh," moaned Katie, staring at the two wet feet she'd lifted from the stream. "My toes! They've been in the water so long, they look like raisins."

"Your big toes look more like prunes," Abby chuckled. "Just stuff them in your boots, and let's go. I'm starving."

The picnic was a sumptuous spread of chicken and vegetables and freshly baked breads and two kinds of pie for dessert. After the meal, Mr. Montgomery and his sons entertained the guests with music. The father played guitar, Mark the fiddle, and Luke an old squeeze box. John's instruments were two metal spoons, which he clacked together against his knee with astonishing speed and rhythm. Their concert included lively country tunes that Vi had often heard before, and when they finished, Mr. Montgomery announced that he'd found a new partner who had agreed to join him for a traditional song.

He took up his guitar again and softly plucked its strings. And Mrs. O'Flaherty began to sing. Her voice was a deep contralto beautifully suited to the old Irish ballad. When she finished, her listeners sat silent for several moments, caught up in the song, until Mr. Montgomery began to clap. They all joined his applause, and the boys loosed their tongues with piercing whistles and boisterous shouts of "Hurrah!"

Mrs. O'Flaherty smiled graciously and agreed without hesitation to an encore—a rousing Irish dance tune to which all the picnickers sang the refrain.

They could have gone on for hours, but Mr. Montgomery reminded the boys that the cows were waiting. Lottie, Mrs. O'Flaherty, and the girls immediately began

helping Mrs. Montgomery clear the table and carry the left-overs, of which there were very few, to the house, while Richard and Mr. Montgomery headed in the direction of the barn and the Allisons' carriage.

The sun was just going down when they departed. On her lap, Lottie carefully held a fresh berry pie, which Mrs. Montgomery had made for Aunt Wealthy. No one talked much on the ride home; it was enough to savor the day.

CHAPTER

4

Life Stories

For everything that was written in the past was written to teach us.

ROMANS 15:4

he following day, being the Sabbath, was subdued but busy. Vi enjoyed her first service at Aunt Wealthy's church, where she met more of Aunt Wealthy's friends. Although the church was only a few blocks from Wealthy's house, Simon drove them in the buggy, and with infinite care, he escorted Wealthy to her pew. The service itself was familiar to Vi from her own church, and Reverend Swift delivered an interesting sermon on the day's text.

The pastor, his wife and daughter, and Mayor and Mrs. Castle were Aunt Wealthy's guests for Sunday dinner. After the delicious meal—the joint effort of Phyllis and Mrs. O'Flaherty—the older people adjourned to the parlor. But Vi and Constance Swift decided to take a stroll about the neighborhood.

Constance was well acquainted with the history of Lansdale and regaled Vi with fascinating stories about the people who lived there and their efforts to transform their town into a modern and progressive city. Constance talked about the new train station and the new gaslights that were being installed in the city's new public park. She took special pride in describing the new public high school, which she attended, and explained that it was the first high school in the region.

When Vi asked about the Swifts' church, Constance told her of the Bible study group that the young ladies of the congregation had formed.

"We're meeting at my house next week, and I'd really like you to come. I can get you after school, and we'll walk together," Constance said excitedly. "You've met most of the girls already, and I know you'll like the ones you haven't been introduced to yet."

"I'd love to join you," Vi said, "but I should check with Aunt Wealthy."

They were just approaching Wealthy's house, so Constance said, "No time like the present! See, she's sitting there on the porch with my parents."

They hurried forward, and soon they had Wealthy's permission for Vi to attend the meeting.

Wealthy was the perfect hostess, but her guests sensed that she was becoming fatigued and soon took their leave. The Swifts were walking down the path to the street when Constance ran back to the porch. "Thank you for letting Vi join us, Miss Stanhope," she said with a happy smile. And to Vi, she added, "We're studying the story of the Prodigal Son. I'll be here Tuesday at four o'clock. Don't forget!"

"She is a charming girl," Wealthy said as she watched Constance run to catch up with her parents. "I knew her great-grandparents and grandparents. I remember chasing our distinguished pastor out of my chicken coop when he was a rascally boy of ten," she added with a chuckle. "You can't imagine how good it feels to see you and his daughter becoming friends, my dear."

Wealthy put her small hand over Vi's and said in a soft and wistful way, "Lansdale is growing very rapidly, Vi, and in some ways, I'm glad I will be going on before it becomes a big city with so many residents that one cannot know them all. Some people still wonder why I chose to live here by myself all these years, but I could never leave. The people of Lansdale have been as close as family to me. Like all families, we have our differences. But we look out for one another and love one another. I thank God every day that He has blessed me with so many good and faithful friends."

Wealthy's smile returned, and she said, "Now you are getting to know Constance and the other young people, so God has blessed me doubly. And soon all my family and friends will be gathered around me—right here in Lansdale."

It had been a long day, and Aunt Wealthy retired immediately after a light supper and prayers with Vi and Mrs. O'Flaherty. Phyllis helped Wealthy to bed and then left to attend evening service at the church.

"Are you sure you didn't want to go to church, Mrs. O?" Vi asked when Phyllis had gone.

"Not this evening," Mrs. O'Flaherty said. "I thought that you and I might have some time together. These past few days have been so busy that I've had no chance to ask about your impressions."

They settled down comfortably in Aunt Wealthy's quaint living room, Vi on the sofa and Mrs. O'Flaherty in an arm chair.

"So tell me. What do you think of Lansdale?" the older woman inquired.

"It's not at all like home," Vi began, "but in a good way. There's a kind of freedom here that's different. I mean, the way most people seem to mix together without worrying about who does what or has what."

"Your Aunt Wealthy surely makes no distinctions, I've noticed," Mrs. O'Flaherty smiled.

"Isn't she grand?" Vi declared.

"I've known duchesses who were not half so grand nor a fraction so wise and good as your aunt."

"Really, Mrs. O'Flaherty—you've known duchesses?" Vi asked in surprise.

"Indeed, and dukes and barons and the occasional prince and princess. And none could hold a candle to Miss Stanhope."

Vi was flabbergasted by her companion's words. "But how…when…?" she stammered.

"How what?" Mrs. O'Flaherty said with a straight face.

"Dukes and duchesses and princes…"

"Oh, they're all over the place where I come from," Mrs. O'Flaherty replied with a wry little smile.

"Did you work for a duchess?" Vi asked.

"No, dear girl," said Mrs. O'Flaherty. She paused for effect before adding, "I nearly was one."

"I knew it!" Vi declared. "I knew there had to be something very exciting in your past!" Then Vi realized what she had said, and her face burned with shame. "Oh, I'm so sorry, Mrs. O'Flaherty. Your past is no business of mine, and I have no right to speculate about you or anyone else."

Mrs. O'Flaherty smiled broadly now. "Apology accepted. But you need not be embarrassed. I have no secrets. I'm well aware that you and the others have an interest in me, for I heard many hints dropped when you were all at Viamede last summer."

Vi lowered her head, because when it came to letting curiosity get the best of good manners, she had been as guilty as anyone.

Mrs. O'Flaherty went on, "I like directness, yet no one save young Herbert asked me straight out. By chance, do you by remember our first meeting?"

Vi looked up and replied, "Herbert asked if you were a pirate."

Mrs. O'Flaherty laughed again. "Oh, how I wish I could have told him that I was. It would have made your brothers so happy to learn that I had lived as a swashbuckler under the skull and crossbones. But alas, my life has not been that colorful."

Vi said, "Your gold tooth made him think that you were like a character in a pirate story. I am sorry for hinting, Mrs. O'Flaherty. Mamma often reminds me of what happened to the curious cat."

"Well, we cannot allow that to happen to you, can we?" Mrs. O'Flaherty teased. "So I shall save you from dying of curiosity—if you would still like to hear my story."

Vi smiled and said, "I would, for I am sure it is most interesting."

"You can only judge that after the hearing. I do not often tell it, for in the telling, it now sounds to me more like one of the melodramatic tales in the dime magazines that are so popular now. You must promise to stop me if I become boring."

"I promise," Vi said, knowing full well that no story of Mrs. O'Flaherty's could ever be boring.

Mrs. O'Flaherty settled back in her chair, and as Vi watched, the woman's face seemed to change—to relax in a way that made her appear almost girlish. Perhaps it was a trick of the light, but her blue eyes seemed to glisten like a many-faceted sapphire.

"I'll begin where all good tales begin," Mrs. O'Flaherty said. "Once upon a time I was not a housekeeper. I was born in a castle—not a very big one, but a castle nevertheless—on a large estate in one of the wild and most beautiful counties of Eire. I am the only daughter of a family of the landed gentry, and I understood very early that my parents and my two older brothers doted on me. My childhood was very happy, in part because no one ever refused me anything. The truth, Vi dear, is that I was pampered most dreadfully, and while I don't believe that I was a bad child, I was willful. Nothing that I experienced taught me that what I wanted might not always be the best thing for me.

"My parents saw that I was educated well. I loved the outdoors, and my father taught me to ride almost as soon as I could walk. I was jumping my pony before I was five, and when I could ride a full-sized horse, my brothers taught me to hunt. I also enjoyed my schoolwork, and I had excellent governesses and tutors when I was growing up. But my mother, who was a fine pianist, saw to my music lessons herself. She was the first to realize that I had some talent for singing."

"More than some talent," Vi interjected. "You have a wonderful voice."

"Thank you kindly. I don't sing as often as I'd like these days. My mother trained me for many years, but when I was sixteen, she engaged a tutor—a young man who was Irish by birth but had studied in London. He came to live at Chanticleer—that was the name of my home. I soon discovered that his true ambition was to be a great composer. But he was poor, and teaching the spoiled daughter of a wealthy family was a means to an end for him."

Mrs. O'Flaherty shifted a bit in the chair, then continued, "My tutor was eight years older than I, and I thought him the most handsome and exciting young man I'd ever laid eyes on. Remember that I was only sixteen, a little older than you are now, and quite sheltered from the real world. You've read novels by Charlotte Brontë, Vi. Based on your knowledge of *Jane Eyre* and *The Professor*, what do you think happened?"

Vi instinctively knew. "You fell in love with your tutor," she said.

"Like an apple falls from the tree," Mrs. O'Flaherty agreed. "That is hardly a novelty. But the wonder was that he loved me as well. Being a willful girl and accustomed to having my way, I saw no difficulty in telling my parents that I had found my heart's desire and intended to marry him."

"And was he?" Vi asked. "Was he your true heart's desire?"

"He was," Mrs. O'Flaherty said. She paused for several moments, and a faraway look came to her blue eyes. Vi could barely contain herself, but she held her tongue until Mrs. O'Flaherty resumed, "Yet he was hardly the choice my parents had in mind. In fact, they had already decided on my future husband. He was the eldest son of an English duke. Our two families had known each other for generations, and this boy had been my playmate. He was gentle and bookish, and I liked him very much. In time, he would inherit his father's title, and if we were married, I would have become a duchess. From my parents' viewpoint, it was a perfect match, for it would unite both families and fortunes."

"But you didn't love this boy," Vi remarked.

"I loved him as a friend, though I'd never have married him. But in the upper classes of most societies, marriages are often like contracts between businesses, and the feelings of the couple take second place. Even in this enlightened year of 1879, Vi, arranged marriages take place among the wealthy and powerful. One of the reasons I have such respect for your own mother is that she so completely supports your sister and her fiancé. Not every woman in Mrs. Travilla's position would welcome a poor artist as a son-in-law.

49

"I was not so fortunate as your sister. I would gladly have waited to marry my tutor until I was older. I thought that would be a reasonable concession. But my father and mother were outraged—something I had never seen before—and they made it clear that no compromise was possible. My tutor was immediately banished from Chanticleer and told never to return to the county. My parents assumed that without his presence, I would soon come to my senses. But I didn't."

Strangely, this memory made Mrs. O'Flaherty smile.

"Love will find a way," she continued. "To make a long story short, I secretly corresponded with him for more than a year. Then with the aid of a sympathetic servant, I left my home and was reunited with my tutor. Just as in a romance novel, we were wed, and I shed the name of my proud family to become Mrs. Ian O'Flaherty. We went immediately to London and took rooms in a house in an area where many impoverished young artists lived, but I was too much in love to realize that we were poor. Naively, I was confident that my parents would relent once they understood how happy I was, so I wrote and asked them to forgive me for eloping and to accept my husband into the family. But to my utter astonishment, they gave me neither forgiveness nor acceptance. My father wrote back that the only way I could return to my family was to give up my husband. My parents had already arranged to have the marriage annulled, and they were sending my brothers to retrieve me, for I had foolishly included the address of our lodgings in my letter. My father made clear that if I failed to obey his instructions, I would be cut off entirely from any inheritance.

"I might have continued my efforts to make peace, but a second letter arrived—this one from my elder brother to my husband. It was not a threat, which I might have expected. It was much worse. My brother offered my dear Ian a very large sum of money to leave me and let the marriage be dissolved."

Vi gasped, "That's awful! As if you were goods to be bought and sold. But what did your husband do?"

"First, he tore the letter to shreds. Then he told me to pack my bags. We left that house an hour later, and we were in Paris by the time my brothers arrived in London to take me back to Ireland."

"But did your family ever relent?" Vi asked. She was thinking how she would feel to be cut off entirely from her mother and her brothers and sisters. Just the idea was painful, and she couldn't imagine such loss.

"No, they didn't," Mrs. O'Flaherty said, her face altering once again. Her eyes lost their glow, and the wrinkles about her mouth reappeared. Her shoulders sagged slightly as if a burden had been placed on her back. "I wrote to my parents occasionally, but they never replied. When they died some years ago, I wrote to my brothers. I asked only to share their sorrow, but I got no response."

Tears had come to Vi's eyes, and she said, "Oh, please, don't go on, Mrs. O'Flaherty. This is too hurtful for you."

Mrs. O'Flaherty looked at Vi and smiled warmly. "You're right, girl, that some memories do hurt, but they hurt more if one always buries them inside. It saddens me that I never reconciled with my family. But I don't regret my marriage, for Ian and I loved one another until the day he died. From him, I learned the real happiness that comes from putting the needs of others before my own selfish desires. And, my girl, we had some glorious times together! My comfort now is knowing that we'll be together again, and that will be the most glorious day of all. That's God's promise to us."

Violet's Amazing Summer

She leaned forward and in a serious tone, she added, "I do not mean to set an example, Vi girl, for I cannot recommend marrying as young as I did. Not by any means. Had I been more mature, I might have been able to convince my family of the rightness of my decision and avoid a permanent break with them. But what's past cannot be undone. Yet it remains one of the real sorrows of my life. To have lost my parents' affection was a heavy price to pay."

At just that moment, the clock on the mantel chimed, and Mrs. O'Flaherty looked up. "Goodness, it's half-past eight and Phyllis will be home at any minute," she said. "I promised to have tea ready. Would you like a cup with us?"

"Yes, please," Vi replied. "And thank you for telling me about your life. It wasn't at all melodramatic. Would it be rude for me to ask to hear more about you and Mr. O'Flaherty?"

Mrs. O'Flaherty stood and fluffed the pillow on the chair. "I should like to tell you about my husband. He was a wonderful man, and it feels good to share my memories of him. You are a very good listener, Violet Travilla. Did you know that?"

"I never even thought of it," Vi confessed, smiling at the compliment. "So you will tell me more?"

"I shall. But not tonight. I think we had best get to bed early, for our days as honored guests are at an end. Tomorrow, Phyllis will put us to work. I have volunteered us for dusting and cleaning and whatever else is needed."

Vi replied that she was ready for any task.

"Good," Mrs. O'Flaherty said. "We can start now. You put the kettle on and get the tea things, and I will prepare toast. I happened to notice a nice pot of homemade blackberry jam in the pantry."

CHAPTER

5

Housecleaning

She sets about her work vigorously; her arms are strong for her tasks.

PROVERBS 31:17

Housecleaning

*M*rs. O'Flaherty was as good as her word, and the next day after breakfast, she and Phyllis outfitted Vi with an apron, a dust cloth, and a gingham kerchief to cover her hair.

"But what is there to clean?" Vi asked. "This house is spotless."

"*No* house is spotless, Miss Vi," Phyllis said. "A person can start at the very top and work her way to the very bottom, and by the time she gets the last speck of dirt gone, it's time to go back to the top and start over again."

Vi laughed merrily and asked, "Are we starting at the top today?"

"I have something else for you and Maureen," Phyllis replied. "You know that your family will be staying here with us for the big doings. Your mother will be in the bedroom next to you, and your little sister and brother in the other upstairs room. We'll get to those later in the week. But come here, girl, and look out the back door. See that little cottage over there? Way in back behind the trees."

Vi had noticed the small white structure during her first walk in the garden, but thinking it to be a storage shed, she hadn't paid it much attention.

"We used to keep chickens, but Miss Wealthy gave 'em up some years back. And bless her for it 'cause I was getting a might old to be chasing hens round the yard. She had the coop torn down and that little house built in its place. It's the guest cottage. It's got two bedrooms and what passes for a sitting room. And that's where your brothers will sleep. It's been awhile since we had guests, so we use it for storage. Today you're going to box up everything, and

Simon will take it all up to the attic where it should've gone in the first place."

"But where is my sister to stay?" Vi wondered. "My big sister, Missy?"

"She'll be over at the Allisons' house, along with your grandparents. Miss Lottie has planned it all out with Miss Wealthy, and they got a place for everybody. Simon was in the Army, you know, and he says that this reunion reminds him of how the generals would station the troops before a battle."

Ten minutes later, Vi and Mrs. O'Flaherty were in the cottage, and Vi realized that even her capable companion was somewhat taken aback by the job ahead of them. Each of the three small rooms was piled with things—blankets and books, old cooking pans and canning jars, broken baskets and picture frames without pictures, odd pieces of furniture that obviously didn't belong. There were old trunks and cases stacked almost to the ceiling in one of the bedrooms, and in the other what seemed to be a mountain of colorful fabrics. Piles of newspapers and magazines dotted the floors in every room.

Mrs. O'Flaherty stood in the tiny hallway that separated the two bedrooms. She squared her broad shoulders, placed her fists on her hips, and said, "Phyllis told me that your aunt was a bit of a packrat, and I will have to compliment her on her powers of understatement."

Mrs. O'Flaherty looked first to her left, into the room with the trunks, then to the room on her right, then back again to the left.

"I believe we should begin by sorting out the luggage," she declared. "If any of those trunks and bags are empty, we can pack them with other things. Young Vi, today you are going to get a lesson in housekeeping. And the first rule is to organize."

"Well," Vi said as she stared at the chaos all about her, "my Papa always said that experience is the best teacher, though how we shall get this place clean, I can't guess."

"We do it by taking one thing at a time," Mrs. O'Flaherty declared with ringing confidence. "Start with just one task and see it through to completion. Then start another. That's how progress is achieved and how housekeepers are made happy."

Most of the bags and valises were empty, so they carried them outside, dusted them off, shook them out, and lined them up on the lawn—ready to be filled. Under the pile of bags were three large trunks and one battered travel case. Two of the trunks were empty, so together, the woman and the girl lifted each in turn, took them outside, and cleaned them. The third trunk was full of items wrapped in wrinkled brown paper. Vi grabbed the leather handle at one end of the trunk and tried to lift it—with much effort but no success.

"Umph!" she exclaimed. "It weighs a ton!"

"Then we'll wait for Simon to help us move it," said Mrs. O'Flaherty. "Now what is in this travel case?"

Vi lifted the top of the square leather box and looked inside. "Just some old letters." She picked up several of the yellowed envelopes and examined them. "They're addressed to Aunt Wealthy. 'In care of Stuart Keith, Esquire, Pleasant Plains, Indiana.' These are letters she must have received when she visited her family there. She told me about it the other night—living on the frontier and helping the Keiths through their first winter. That was back about the time my mother was born, in the 1830s."

Mrs. O'Flaherty looked at the worn envelopes and faded writing and said, "We should put these in a place safe from hungry insects. I have a feeling we may find more such treasures for safekeeping. Vi, will you look for a box that we can use temporarily for special things?"

Vi located an empty wooden box and placed the letters in it. She could see now that the room was a charming sleeping area with a wide iron bed, a dresser, and a wash stand. The room was still cluttered, but in less than an hour, they had made considerable progress.

At Mrs. O'Flaherty's suggestion, Vi continued to work on this room while Mrs. O'Flaherty started clearing the other bedroom. Vi stripped the bed of its covers and took the feather pillows, which she'd found under a jumble of old clothing, out to air. She sorted the clothes into piles and packed them into boxes. Under the bed, she found a collection of shoes and boots. Those that had laces were tied together, so Vi slung these pairs over her arms and carried them to the lawn. Soon a small army of footwear appeared to be marching in file away from the little cottage.

Then Vi tackled the dresser. Each drawer was full of things—from old pincushions to a basket of seashells to children's toys in need of repair. Most of these things she put in one of the crates supplied by Simon, but for some reason, she decided to include the prettiest of the shells in the safekeeping box.

She was pushing the bottom drawer back into place when she heard a sound, like bumping, from behind the dresser. She jumped back, thinking it might be a mouse, and listened. No further noise. She gave the dresser a slight shove, and the bumping sounded again. *Mice scurry but they don't bump*, she assured herself, and she carefully shifted the dresser away from the wall.

Housecleaning

Another bump came, and Vi peered into the narrow space she'd created between the dresser and the wall. She could just make out a square-ish shape in the shadow, and she thought it might be a book. So she reached for it. She'd guessed wrong. It was a picture frame, and its glass was intact but so covered with grime that she couldn't tell if there was a picture.

With her dust cloth, she rubbed at the glass and a face began to emerge—a girl's face drawn in pencil or charcoal. *It might be someone Aunt Wealthy knows*, Vi thought. *Maybe someone who is coming to the reunion. I'll put this in the safekeeping box.*

After another hour, Vi realized that the room was indeed neat, and ready to be cleaned.

"Ah, you are a bit ahead of me," said Mrs. O'Flaherty as she entered and surveyed the room. "This looks grand," she said admiringly. "This room will suit the twins, for the bed in the other room is only large enough for one. You've done an excellent job, Vi. Now, do you want to help me or start on the sitting room?"

Vi considered. "If I help you, we can finish faster. Then we'll have two rooms completed before lunch."

"You're thinking like a housekeeper, my girl," Mrs. O'Flaherty smiled.

They did indeed make short work of the second bedroom. Mrs. O'Flaherty had been sorting and folding the fabrics that had engulfed the room like a tidal wave.

"There are enough remnants here to make a hundred quilts," Mrs. O'Flaherty said. "And some pieces are quite beautiful, in patterns I haven't seen for years. Your aunt must have been collecting this material for a very long time."

"Phyllis said that Aunt Wealthy used to sew clothes for children," Vi said.

"That explains this," Mrs. O'Flaherty commented as she lifted a sheet from something under the window and displayed an old sewing machine. "Do you know that when your mother and I were children, every stitch we wore had to be sewn by hand? There were no shops that sold new clothing already made. We had a seamstress, and I remember her sitting by the fire in the kitchen, late into the night. At the time I thought her quite elderly, but she was probably about the age I am now. And her hands always seemed to be flying, in and out, in and out, over some rich fabric that would become a beautiful dress for my mother or me. This woman herself was always attired in the simplest dark calico." Mrs. O'Flaherty paused and shook her head in a sad gesture. "To make her living, she made other women beautiful, but I doubt she ever had a pretty dress for herself. I don't think I knew her name, but I know now that she was 'clothed in strength and dignity,' as it says in Proverbs. It took me many years to understand that strength and dignity are precious. 'Charm is deceptive, and beauty is fleeting; but a woman who fears the LORD is to be praised.'"

Mrs. O'Flaherty worked as she talked, and she told Vi more about her life at Chanticleer. They'd just finished when Mrs. O'Flaherty said, "Praising others comes hard for me, probably because it was never expected of me as a child. But I must tell you, Vi, that you are earning my respect more and more each day. No—no. Don't lower your head like that. It's important to learn to accept praise when it is deserved. Everyone needs to know when she or he is doing something well. I am inclined to be stingy with my compliments, but I tell you, Vi girl, that you impress me.

I like the way you learn from others and then take the bull by the horns—I believe that is the saying—and use your head to get the job done in the best way. You've got a good head on your shoulders—the kind that knows the value of a compliment and doesn't get puffed up with pride."

Flushing with pleasure, Vi said, "Thank you, Mrs. O'Flaherty, for your words. And thank you also for making me think. That is something I miss most about Papa. He always made me think."

Mrs. O'Flaherty was filling her arms with bundles of cloth. "I have heard your father described as a person who was never fearful of asking difficult questions and searching until he found the right answers, even if the search was painful. I begin to see that his legacy was passed on."

With that, she vanished out the door. Vi followed with her own armload, and it was not long before they had filled the two empty trunks and the travel case with Aunt Wealthy's remnants. And soon they had completed clearing the second bedroom.

They returned to the cottage after lunch, and finished the little sitting room by mid-afternoon. Simon joined them and with his help, they took the mattresses outside for airing and packed empty cartons and crates with all the things they had removed from the house. Later in the afternoon, Vi was surprised to see Mark and Luke Montgomery arrive. They had been recruited by Mr. Allison, who had learned about the cottage cleaning from Aunt Wealthy.

"Just what we needed!" Mrs. O'Flaherty declared as the boys approached the cottage. "You are 'the strength God provides,'" she added, quoting from 1 Peter.

The daylight was fading when the last of the containers was removed to Aunt Wealthy's attic and the mattresses returned to their beds. All that remained was the wooden box of treasures, which Vi carried to the house and quickly stored on the floor of the kitchen pantry.

Invited to stay for supper, the Montgomery boys thanked Miss Stanhope but said they must be going home. Phyllis wouldn't let them leave until they accepted a basket of her famous biscuits for their family.

When Vi entered the kitchen, Phyllis said, "I've drawn you a tub of hot water to wash off all that dust. You aren't so accustomed to such lifting and toting as you've done today, and a good soak will take the kinks out."

"Phyllis is right," said Mrs. O'Flaherty, who was looking forward to a thorough washing herself. "You want to be in good shape tomorrow. We straightened the cottage today, but first thing in the morning, we start to clean it stem to stern."

Vi needed little convincing. At that moment, there was nothing in the world she wanted more than a hot bath.

The next day they worked harder than ever—washing walls and windows, sweeping and scrubbing floors, and polishing the sparse furniture in the little house. Phyllis used both her new ringer machine and her old kettle to wash the bed linens, and Simon took the cottage's braided rugs out to the mown field at the rear of Aunt Wealthy's property. Spreading them over the dry grass, he beat each rug with a wire implement until the last particle of dust and dirt was shaken free.

Vi was indeed glad she'd had that long, hot bath the previous evening, for her shoulders and neck were somewhat stiff when she awoke. The physical sensation, she thought, was like the way she felt whenever she rode her horse again after a summer holiday away from Ion. When she had complained about her aches, her father explained that muscles in the human body will rebel when they are put to use after long periods of idleness. "What is true of arms and legs and shoulders," he'd said, "applies as well to the brain. When people say that it hurts to think, it is often because they are unused to exercising their mental abilities."

Vi had always been expected to help at home, as were all her siblings, but she had never before done the kind of heavy housework she was doing now. As she washed and polished and swept cobwebs from the ceilings, she thought of something else her father had said. Whether humble or lofty, all work that is done for the glory of God and the benefit of one's fellow humans has dignity and should be honored.

It was close to three in the afternoon when Mrs. O'Flaherty stopped Vi as the girl was cutting fresh lining paper for the dresser drawers. "It's time to put your tools down," Mrs. O'Flaherty said.

At Vi's quizzical look, Mrs. O'Flaherty asked, "Have you forgotten that you have an engagement? Miss Constance Swift will be coming at four to escort you to the Bible study meeting."

Vi had forgotten, and she almost wanted to skip the gathering. But Mrs. O'Flaherty assured her that the work on the cottage was nearly done. "Go on now, and dress. I'll finish those drawers, and then I, too, shall rest my weary bones. Tomorrow we will make the beds and hang the curtains, and Simon will lay the rugs. Then we can close the cottage door till the twins and Ed arrive."

Violet's Amazing Summer

With some reluctance, Vi returned to the house to make herself ready. So she missed seeing the broad smile that broke out on Mrs. O'Flaherty's face. *As the Americans say, that girl's got grit*, the older woman thought. *I never knew a girl her age so ready for new challenges. She doesn't know what she's capable of yet, but someday, she's going to make her mark on this world. Watch over her, Lord, and keep her strong. Whatever Your plan for her might be, help her stay strong in body and spirit.*

The little cottage now empty, Mrs. O'Flaherty felt free to lift her powerful voice in a hymn of praise as she finished her work.

In the end, Vi was grateful to Mrs. O'Flaherty for remembering the Bible study meeting, for it proved to be a most enlightening afternoon. Constance's mother had prepared a delicious tea for the young ladies, and then proved herself to be a wise parent by absenting herself from the meeting.

Vi had met most of the group before, and she was quickly introduced to those she didn't know. She had thought that Katie Allison and Abby Montgomery might be there, but Amy Fletcher explained that the group was formed for girls of high school age and older: "Katie and Abby and several more will join us next year, when they are fourteen."

The text for discussion was the parable of the lost son in Chapter fifteen of the book of Luke. The girls talked enthusiastically about the greater meaning of the father's forgiveness of his errant son and God's forgiveness of all who seek Him regardless of their sins.

The discussion went on until six o'clock, when Mrs. Swift entered the sitting room and graciously but firmly declared the meeting at an end. "I am sure you young ladies could continue your conversation for an hour more, but suppertime is near, and some of you also have homework to attend to."

The girls, after saying a prayer and thanking Constance and her mother, left together. They walked down the broad street and chatted gaily, and Vi began to feel as if she'd know all these girls for years—not just the week since her arrival in Lansdale.

Supper was ready when she reached the Stanhope house, and Vi hurried to join her aunt and Mrs. O'Flaherty at the table.

"I hope you enjoyed the study Bible meeting," Wealthy said.

"Yes, ma'am, very much," Vi replied. "We had a good discussion about the parable of the prodigal son, though it turned into a conversation about brothers and sisters and getting along with them."

"Ah, that can be a vexing problem at times," Wealthy said with a little smile. "It is not always easy to keep your brother, or sister."

Vi, who hardly even noticed her aunt's odd speech by now, understood the reference to the story of Cain and Abel.

"And did you enjoy being with the young ladies?" Wealthy asked.

"Oh, I did," Vi replied happily. "They're such nice girls and each one so interesting in her own way. I realized as we were walking home that I really haven't known many girls my own age before."

"That's probably because you are a country girl and educated at home," Wealthy said. "You do not have the same opportunities to mix and mingle as if you lived in a town or a city."

They all went back to their meal for several minutes, and then Vi asked, "I know that you lived with the Keiths in Indiana, Aunt Wealthy, but have you been many other places?"

This question drew a wide smile from the elderly lady. "Oh, my dear Vi, when I was a girl, I loved to travel. Journeys abroad were not so easy then, but my father and stepmother—who was your great-great-grandmother—took me to many places in our country. One trip I remember most fondly was a visit to Nantucket when I was just a little older than you. My father was a merchant in whale oil and many other things, and he wanted me to see where the oil came from. Of course, the oil came from whales, and I didn't see a whale. But I saw the brave men who caught them. Caught the whales, I mean. I can recall walking along the water's edge and seeing the whaling ships. One of the sailors gave me a bone he'd made."

Wealthy's memory triggered Vi's, and the girl sprang up from the table. "Excuse me just a moment," she said. "I'll be right back." And she hurried to the kitchen.

Vi returned in no more than a minute, a small wooden box clutched in her hands. She placed the box beside Wealthy's place on the table.

"I almost forgot this," Vi explained. "We collected some special things in the cottage and put them here for you, Aunt Wealthy. When you said 'bone,' I remembered that I'd found something like that and put it in this box. I thought it might be ivory."

She reached into the box and retrieved an item that looked like a hard white stone, carved with an intricate picture of a sailing ship. Wealthy took the piece, which just fit her small palm, and stared at it for several moments.

"I haven't seen this in ages," Wealthy said. "Thank you, my dear, for this is the very piece of bone the Nantucket seaman gave me. He had made this etching of his ship during one of his voyages."

"I believe that such whalebone carvings are called 'scrimshaw,'" Mrs. O'Flaherty commented.

"What an unusual word," Aunt Wealthy said. "I must remember to remember it."

She began poking around in the box, examining each item and telling something of its origin. The seashell, she said, had come from a trip with her father to the islands of the Caribbean. There was a brass belt buckle that had belonged to Harry Duncan, and a pair of white lace gloves that Wealthy remembered wearing to Elsie and Edward Travilla's wedding. Wealthy had a story for everything in the box, but when she came to the letters near the bottom, she could not speak at first.

Slowly, she examined the envelopes, running her thin fingers over the writing on the fronts. "These are treasures," she said at last, "for every one contains a message from the past. After all these years, I still recognize each hand, though the writers long ago made their final journey to our Heavenly Father."

Wealthy looked up, and behind her aunt's little spectacles, Vi saw tears.

"Oh, dear," Wealthy said, sniffling slightly. "These have made me sentimental. But it is so good to remember old friends and to think that I shall be seeing them again soon."

"Not so soon," Vi protested.

"No," Wealthy smiled, "but soon enough. God has granted me an abundance of years—many more than my allotted three score and ten, as Psalm 90 says—but I know that His call is not far away. At my age, dear child, there is comfort and joy in that thought. Life has always been a great adventure for me, but it is only a prelude to the glorious adventure ahead."

"Would you like to read those letters now?" Mrs. O'Flaherty asked.

"Later," Wealthy replied as she gathered the envelopes and put them into her pocket. "Perhaps I shall read one a day. There are enough here to take me to my birthday. But, Vi, are these the last in the box?"

Vi looked inside and saw only the dirt-covered picture frame. "There's one more item, but it needs a cleaning before we can see what it is," she said.

Phyllis had just come in and was clearing the supper dishes. "Bring that filthy thing into the kitchen, and we'll have it clean right quick," she said. "While we're washing, Maureen can help Wealthy to the sitting room."

In the kitchen, Phyllis got a soft rag and poured some vinegar on it. "Rub the glass gently, Vi, and the dirt will come off."

Vi worked carefully, and Phyllis watched over her shoulder. As the drawing came clear, Phyllis said, "It looks kinda like Wealthy, but not exactly. I don't think she ever had curls like that."

When the glass was sparkling, Vi removed as much dirt as she dared from the delicate frame and dusted the backing. A date had been written there — 1814.

When Vi presented the picture to her aunt, Wealthy gazed at it as she had at the envelopes. There were no tears this time, but a brilliant smile seemed to illuminate her face.

"Is it you?" Phyllis asked, getting right to the point.

"No," Wealthy replied, "for I was a rather plain girl. But I take your question as a compliment, Phyllis. This is my little sister and Vi's great-grandmother — Eva Violet Stanhope, who married Horace Dinsmore, Sr."

"My Grandpapa's mother," Vi said softly. Looking more closely at the face of the young woman in the picture, she began to see the resemblance to her grandfather — the shape of the nose, the curve of the eyebrows, the set of the chin.

"Indeed, and a sweeter young woman never was," Wealthy was saying. "Eva was nineteen or twenty when this drawing was made, in the youth of her bloom. I remember that this picture was done shortly before her wedding. How could I ever have misplaced it?"

Wealthy regarded the picture for some minutes more, then she said, "Phyllis, will you find this drawing a place of honor on the mantel? We shall keep it there while Violet is our guest. And when you leave us, Vi, I want you to take your great-grandmother's image as my birthday present to you."

"But you must keep it, Aunt Wealthy," Vi insisted.

"I have Eva and my other sisters always with me, child, in my memories. But you never had the chance to know her, so this drawing will stand instead. I will tell you more about her, and you can look at her picture and put a face to my stories."

"But not tonight," Phyllis said firmly. "It's time we get you ready for bed, Wealthy."

"You're like a mother hen the way you brood over me," Wealthy said with a girlish little giggle, as Phyllis took her arm and helped her to rise.

They were almost at the doorway when Wealthy stopped and turned back.

"Vi, dear, please put that sheepshank on the mantel as well, will you?"

"Yes, ma'am," Vi agreed with a grin. Bidding her aunt good night once more, Vi went to the dining table to get the *scrimshaw* — and heard low, rich laughter behind her.

"Your aunt is the real treasure in this house," Mrs. O'Flaherty said. "And had it not been for you, my girl, I should never have met her."

CHAPTER

6

Anticipated Arrivals

Greet one another with a kiss of love.

1 PETER 5:14

Anticipated Arrivals

From Vi's journal, dated Friday, May 30, 1879:

I received a letter from Mamma today, and she wrote that Cousin James will be coming up from Viamede. Also, Aunt Louise will accompany Great-Grandpa, and Isa will be coming as well! (Before I left Ion, Missy told me a suspicion she has about Isa and Cousin James, but I don't know. I think Missy thinks everyone should be falling in love and getting married like her.) Mamma says that she tried her best to convince Aunt Chloe to join us, but to no avail. Chloe will not spend even a day apart from Joe.

It's too bad that Aunt Rosie can't travel, but her new baby is due in July, and Mamma says that the train ride would be too difficult for her. But Uncle Trip, Aunt Eloise and their children will be here. And Ed is coming directly from the University.

Aunt Wealthy has received acceptances from most of the Keiths. I shall have to work very hard to learn all their names, for there are even more Keiths than Dinsmores and Travillas. Aunt Marcia and Uncle Stuart Keith, who are a few years older than my Grandpapa, have seven grown children, many grandchildren, and even great-grandchildren. I am going to start my list with the names I know so far:

Dr. and Mrs. Charles Landreth—This is our cousin Millie, who is the Keiths' oldest daughter. The Landreths have four children—Percy, who is married, Marcia, Stuart, and Fanny. They're all older than I, but Fanny Landreth is about Missy's age.

Mr. and Mrs. Wallace Ormsby — She is our cousin Zillah, the second Keith daughter. Mr. Ormsby is a lawyer, and they have two children (I think).

Reverend and Mrs. Frank Osbourne — Mrs. Osbourne is Adah, the third Keith daughter. They also have two children. (I must get their names.)

<u>Important note to myself</u>. Dr. and Mrs. Landreth and Reverend and Mrs. Osbourne have all been missionaries overseas. I hope to hear about their experiences.

Mr. Rupert Keith — He's the oldest Keith son, and he met his wife when they were held captive by Indians! (Do they have children? Ask Aunt Wealthy.)

Reverend Cyril Keith — This is Cousin James's father and also a minister. He's a widower.

Mr. Donald Keith — He's Cyril Keith's twin brother. He lives with his family in New Jersey. He won't be able to attend the reunion, but I must remember his name.

I see that I have many more names to fill in, but Aunt Wealthy will help me. Phyllis and Simon, too. It amazes me that my almost 100-year-old aunt can remember everyone, down to the very youngest, and she has wonderful stories about each person. But Aunt Wealthy sympathizes with me. She has advised me never to be embarrassed if I forget someone's name. She said that I should just smile and ask.

Today, Phyllis finally pronounced the house ready for guests, and it does almost shine from top to bottom. Aunt Wealthy told us that she's as "punched as please"

about the house, and we can all see that she is *pleased as punch* about the reunion. Although the housecleaning is over, we will not sit idle. Tomorrow night, Aunt Wealthy and I will dine with the Allisons, and we've been invited to visit the farm again on Sunday, after church. I'm having supper with Constance and her parents after Bible study on Tuesday. Then my family arrives next Thursday! It will be such fun introducing them to all my new friends here.

I realized something about myself today. I have missed Mamma and the others every single day that I've been in Lansdale, yet I haven't felt homesick at all. Isn't that curious? I must ask Mamma about it. I have so many things to tell her.

Vi laid her pen aside and closed her journal. She moved from the little desk to her bed and took up her Bible. She opened to the book of Matthew and turned quickly to the fifteenth chapter. There she read one of her favorite stories, that of Jesus feeding the four thousand.

Vi closed her eyes and spoke from her heart: "Dear Lord, thank You for the gift of Your saving grace. And thank You for the example of Your Son and His compassion for others. Please help me to be more like Him and to put the needs of others before my own. You have enriched my life so much through my Aunt Wealthy and the Gleesons and Mrs. O'Flaherty and everyone I've met in Lansdale. Soon I'll be meeting more people and getting to know family members from many different places. Please watch over everyone and keep them safe during their journeys. And also those who cannot be with us. I know this reunion may be difficult for some, especially Grandpapa and Great-Grandpapa, and they may have special need of Your strength and compassion. Just help them, Dear Lord, to heal old wounds and rejoice in the love of family and friends."

The next four days seemed to fly by. Apart from her social engagements, Vi spent as much time as she could with Wealthy, learning more about the Stanhopes and the Keiths and their family history. But none of the stories meant as much to Vi as those of her great-grandmother Eva.

"I cannot help thinking that your grandfather's life would have been very different had Eva lived," Wealthy said on the day before the arrival of Vi's family. "My sister was a good and loving Christian in the best sense, for she truly lived her faith in everything she did. Nothing could sway her from doing what she knew to be right."

Wealthy went on in a softer tone, "Eva's death was hard for your grandfather, as the loss of a parent always is. But it was harder still on Horace, Sr. He fell away from his faith when Eva died, and without her guidance and support, young Horace Jr. was not raised in true faith."

Vi said, "Grandpapa often says that it was his pride that kept his heart closed for so long."

"That's true," Wealthy agreed. "But not pride alone. Horace, Jr., suffered terribly when his first wife, Elsie Grayson, was taken from him, but he could not admit it to anyone. He made the mistake that many make; he thought that to be strong, he must bear his sorrow alone. That was the real cause of his breach with Marcia and Stuart Keith, who wanted to support him through his pain."

"What did happen, Aunt Wealthy?" Vi asked. "Grandpapa has explained that he rejected the Keiths' offer of help after his wife died, but that doesn't seem enough for so long a separation."

"Horace rejected all offers of help at that time," Aunt Wealthy replied with a little sigh. "Even my own. He resented any suggestion that he turn to the Lord to heal his wounds. Marcia tried many times to contact him during those years, until finally she realized that Horace would have to come to God in his own way. But none of us ever stopped praying for him. We knew his way would be very hard, and it was.

"Your grandfather had loved and lost his mother, and he had loved and lost his young bride. But only when he almost lost his daughter—your dear mother, Elsie—did he open his heart and give his life to our Heavenly Father. For Horace, the door to salvation was opened by his child. But I like to think that somewhere deep inside him, Horace held to the memory of his mother and that Eva's early teachings may have helped him too."

"But the estrangement with the Keiths lasted for so long," Vi said.

"There were other problems, my dear. Your Ohio and Indiana relatives were ardent abolitionists and abhorred slavery. Yet Horace, Sr., and Horace, Jr., were both slaveowners. There were incidents. Oh, there's no need for details. But matters of conscience drove a wedge between the families. That summer when your mother came to visit me here in Lansdale healed any misunderstandings between your grandfather and me. But other things occurred, and then the war came. That awful conflict separated many families. Yet honestly, Vi, I think that the estrangement between the Dinsmores and the Keiths had simply become a habit—a bad habit that Horace broke when he at last wrote to Marcia and Stuart. And their correspondence has led to the family reunion we are preparing for."

Vi didn't press her aunt for more information, for she could tell that Wealthy would rather talk of other memories. So she asked, "How old was Grandpapa when his mother died?"

"Oh, about four or five as I recall," Wealthy replied. "I know that he was old enough to remember her, in the way one remembers a dream, and he missed her greatly. I saw him several times when he was a boy, and he would always beg me to tell him about Eva."

Wealthy looked up at the drawing of her half-sister that now stood on the mantelpiece. "Your grandfather will be happy to see that picture," Wealthy said.

"He might like to have it," Vi suggested.

"Perhaps, but that is your decision, my girl," Wealthy said, "for the drawing is yours. It would please Eva to know that her great-granddaughter is now the keeper of her image. I trust you to make the best use of it. But tell me now what you have planned for this afternoon," the old lady asked.

"If it is all right with you, Aunt Wealthy, I'd like to go to the Allisons. Aunt Lottie is preparing baskets of fresh fruit for all the family who will be staying at hotels. But if you need me. . ."

Wealthy interrupted, "I need you to help Lottie. It is because of her and your Uncle Richard that this reunion is possible. Besides, I plan to take a long nap after lunch, for

I must be as strong as an ox when our guests begin to arrive tomorrow."

"Oh, not an ox," Vi laughed. "I cannot imagine you as an ox, Aunt Wealthy."

"Admittedly a very small ox," her aunt said with a grin. "Perhaps an eagle is a better simile. I cannot fly, but I have decided to wear my feathers and quills tomorrow."

At Vi's questioning look, Wealthy said, "That's all I will say. You will have to wait one more day to see your old aunt in her feathers."

Feathers and quills, however, were the last things on Vi's mind the next morning as she watched the train grinding slowly to a stop. With Katie just a step behind her, Vi trotted along the platform, scanning the windows of the passenger cars for familiar faces. The noise was deafening, and the steam clouded her vision, but still she searched. And she was rewarded at last. It was Rosemary—her nose pressed flat against the window of one of the compartments. Vi waved her arms wildly until she caught her little sister's eye. She saw Rosemary's mouth open wide, and almost instantly, more faces appeared at the window—Harold and Herbert, Danny, and then Grandpapa! Vi's heart pounded with excitement as she waved and shouted her hello's.

"Come along, Vi," said Lottie, who had caught up to the girls. "Let's get to the door of the train car and greet your family."

Vi turned to follow Lottie and nearly tripped over some pieces of luggage as she hurried down the platform. A moment later, she was caught up in her mother's arms.

Then everyone was hugging and laughing. Little Danny clung to Vi's legs until she lifted him in her arms and kissed him thoroughly.

Richard Allison had joined the happy family reunion, and he sought out his sister and brother-in-law, Rose and Horace, for a special greeting. More hugging and hand-shaking followed, and the Allisons and Katie were introduced to the Travilla children.

Looking around her, Vi realized that someone was missing. "Mamma, where's Missy?" she asked anxiously.

"She is coming tomorrow afternoon, with Trip and Eloise and the boys," Elsie said. "We decided not to bring the nursemaids, for there are already so many people that must be accommodated. Your sister offered to help your aunt and uncle with the children."

Vi, who was still holding her little brother, smiled at her mother. "And I can help with you-know-who," she said with a wink.

Danny piped up, "Help with who?"

Vi tickled him gently under his chin, making him giggle, and said, "You, silly. I'll be your nursemaid, and you'll be mine."

When the happy passengers reached the neat brick house on Wealthy's quiet street, the red carpet was out— as Vi already knew, for she had helped Simon lay it down that morning. What she hadn't expected was Aunt Wealthy herself, standing at the top of the porch steps, supported by Mrs. O'Flaherty's strong arm. But the real surprise crowned Wealthy's head. Vi's aunt, though simply gowned, was wearing a strange crown of dark feathers secured to her bun with a buckskin band. The feathers waved slightly every time Wealthy nodded so that her

80

aunt reminded Vi of the stately palm trees she'd seen in New Orleans.

Danny, who was sitting on Vi's lap, whispered, "Is that lady an Indian chief?"

"No, that's your Aunt Wealthy," Vi explained.

"Well, she sure looks like an Indian to me," Danny said uncertainly.

"You're not afraid, are you?" Vi asked.

Danny puffed up his cheeks in an expression of disgust. "Not hardly," he replied with exaggerated firmness. "I like Indians 'cause they're brave and strong."

"Then you'll like Aunt Wealthy because she's very brave. And very kind, too. But she's not so strong, and you must be gentle when you shake hands with her."

"I will," Danny promised. Then he added in a tone that conveyed his wonderment, "I never shaked hands with an Indian chief before."

Soon all the guests were inside, gathered on the sofa and chairs around Wealthy. Phyllis and Simon—after warmly welcoming Elsie, Rose, and Horace and meeting all the children—were passing glasses of lemonade. Mrs. O'Flaherty stayed rather close to Wealthy, assisting her with anything she needed.

"Well, children," Wealthy said as soon as all were served their drinks. "What do you think of my feathers?"

Without a second's hesitation, Danny asked, "Are you an Indian chief?"

"No, young man, I'm not," Wealthy replied, "but I would be very proud if I were. These eagle feathers and porcupine quills were a gift to me from an old woman of the Potawatomi tribe whom I met many, many years ago in Indiana. Long ago, I sewed them to this leather band so that

I could wear them, though this is not a Potawatomi custom. To me, they symbolize goodwill and the friendship of that kind woman, and I am wearing them today because all the people of my family are coming together here in love and goodwill after so many years."

"But we're here for your birthday, Aunt Wealthy," Rosemary said, "and Vi's, too."

"Birthdays are being celebrated too, dear child," Wealthy replied. "And now that you are here, I have part of my birthday present—with more to come today and tomorrow as the rest of the family arrive."

"When do you expect Marcia and Stuart?" Horace asked, for in truth, he anticipated his reunion with his cousin and her husband more than any other aspect of the visit.

"Tomorrow morning, on the first train from the West," Wealthy said.

"I would like to meet them at the station, if that is agreeable," Horace said, and Wealthy assured him it was.

"Now, it is time to get everyone to their places," Wealthy continued. "But if no one minds, I shall only observe." She looked into all the bright young faces about her and added, "It is one of the privileges of my extreme age, children, that I may now rest while others work. And when each of you is a hundred, you will be allowed to sit in your chair."

"And wear feathers?" Danny asked, grinning at the possibility.

"Well, Daniel, when you are a hundred years old, you can wear all the feathers you like," Wealthy asserted. "And no one will say a word about it, even if they think you are quite the oddest sight they've ever seen. Now, Phyllis will show you where everything is. But we have something special in store for your handsome twins. Herbert and Harold, I've asked Vi to be your hostess, so you just follow her now."

The Travilla twins, who had been told nothing of the little guest cottage, looked at Vi in curiosity. But all she said was, "Get your valises, and I'll lead the way."

The Lansdale train depot was more than usually busy that day and the next. By carriage and buggy, the family members were taken to their accommodations, all under the expert direction of Lottie and Richard King.

Ed Travilla arrived the first afternoon and after greeting Aunt Wealthy, he was shown to the little cottage, which the twins were already calling their "bachelor quarters." Horace and Rose were settled comfortably at the Allisons'. A suite of rooms had been reserved at the Lansdale Hotel for Horace Dinsmore, Sr., his daughter Louise Conley, and her daughter Isa. Trip Dinsmore and his young family would also stay at the hotel, as would a number of the Keiths. In fact, both of Lansdale's finest hotels would be filled with members of the Stanhope family, as were several of the town's nicest homes.

"When is the birthday party?" Ed Travilla was asking his mother as they enjoyed a few minutes of quiet together on Wealthy's porch.

"Saturday evening," Elsie responded. "It will be held in the ballroom of the Lansdale Hotel. I don't know exactly what is planned, for both Aunt Wealthy and Lottie are being very secretive, as is our Vi."

"And has my little sister enjoyed her stay here?" Ed inquired.

"Clearly she has," Elsie smiled. "I must confess that I have missed her very much, just as I miss you when you are away at school. But as your father would surely remind me, our fledglings must be allowed to fly on their own wings."

"Is it very hard for you, Mamma?" Ed asked with some concern.

"It is hard not to have you all around me," Elsie said, "but I am more than compensated by the pride I feel in the adults that you and Missy have become. Missing one's grown children is natural, and I will shed tears when Missy marries in December. But never tears of regret, for wherever you go, I know that you are following in Jesus' footsteps and doing what is right."

"Well, I shall be home in another few years," Ed said, "and Vi will not be flying away anytime soon."

"Flying away?" Vi said as she came out onto the porch.

Elsie gestured to her daughter. "Come sit beside me, dear. Ed and I were just talking about how all of you are growing up and how proud I am of you. Mrs. O'Flaherty has told me that you have been of such help to her during your stay here. So tell us all about what you have been up to in Lansdale."

Vi happily obliged, and her mother noticed that for a girl who sometimes had trouble remembering names, Vi had learned a great many in the past month.

7

Birthdays and Messages

*They will celebrate your abundant
goodness and joyfully sing
of your righteousness.*

PSALM 145:7

ose Dinsmore was tying her husband's dress necktie when Horace asked, "Do you think Vi may feel somewhat let down at the party tonight? I'm afraid few people remember that she is to share this birthday celebration with Aunt Wealthy."

"Don't worry, dear," Rose said, giving her husband's crisp, white bow a final pat. "Lottie has something special planned for Vi. And besides, Vi's actual birthday is not for five days yet. I don't believe our granddaughter has any expectation of being the center of attention tonight."

"But we will be en route back to the South on Vi's actual birthday, and a train is hardly the setting for a sweet sixteen party," Horace complained. "Turning sixteen is a big event for a girl."

"And it will be for our Vi," Rose assured him again. "Now step back, and let me inspect my distinguished husband."

Horace did as directed, saying, "I think you know more than you're telling me. I've seen you and Elsie and Lottie with your heads together, and I begin to suspect you are up to something. Can it be that you already know what Lottie has planned?"

There was the faintest hint of mischief in Rose's lovely smile. "Ask me no questions," she replied mysteriously. "It's time we go down to the parlor, for we don't want to detain the departure for the hotel."

"You are avoiding my question," Horace laughed. He looked at his pocket watch. "Lottie and Richard do not expect us in the parlor for another quarter of an hour."

87

"It never hurts to be a little early," Rose said as she gathered her shawl and purse.

"Then you may precede me, dear, for I have something else to attend to before I make my grand entrance," Horace said. "Trip brought some letters from The Oaks when he arrived yesterday, and I have been too occupied to open them. Just business, I imagine, but I should take a look. I will join you downstairs in no more than ten minutes."

Rose came close and kissed his cheek. Then she went to the door of the bedroom they occupied in the Allisons' home, saying, "Don't forget the notes for your tribute," as she left.

Horace went to the nightstand and took up the small pile of letters that he had tossed there the day before. Quickly shuffling through them, he thought that he'd judged correctly—business matters and nothing of urgency. The last envelope, however, puzzled him. The name above the return address was smudged but also familiar. Horace thought it might be "M. Love."

Tearing the envelope open, he removed two sheets of paper and quickly checked the signature at the bottom of the second. "Mitchell Love," he read. "Now what could my old friend be writing to me about? Some interesting news from Rome, I hope."

Without reading more, he returned the letter to the envelope and put it in his breast pocket with the notes for his speech.

The Lansdale Hotel was alive with lights and laughter when Vi arrived with her mother and her brothers and sisters.

They were just in time to see Wealthy Stanhope enter the ballroom on the arm of her nephew Harry Duncan, and to join in the happy cheer that went up from the guests. With Harry's strong arm around her waist, Wealthy moved slowly and regally through the room, greeting everyone, until they came to her place of honor at a long table at the far side.

The cloth-covered table was beautifully decorated with fresh flowers in silver bowls, and Vi observed that there were many smaller dining tables about the room, each decorated in the same fashion. Already seated at Aunt Wealthy's table was Horace Dinsmore, Sr., who with great effort stood to welcome his elderly sister-in-law. May Duncan was there as well, and the table was soon completed by the arrival of Horace and Rose and also Marcia and Stuart Keith and their eldest daughter, Millie Landreth, and her husband.

"Are you sitting with Aunt Wealthy too?" Rosemary whispered to her mother.

"No, dear," Elsie replied. "You, Missy, Danny, and I will be together at a table with Aunt Louise and Cousin Isa. I believe that Cousin James and his father will dine with us as well." She turned to Ed and said, "You and the twins are to sit with Trip and Eloise and the Osbournes."

Listening to her mother, Vi had not heard her own name. "Am I to be at your table, Mamma?" she asked.

"No, not with me, dear," Elsie answered a little absent-mindedly. "Now let me think. Where is Vi to be seated? Do you remember, Missy?"

Gazing around the crowded room, Missy said, "I don't think it was ever mentioned. But there must be a place for Vi somewhere. Do you know, Ed?"

Looking into Vi's anxious eyes, Ed said, "I'll find her a place, though she might have to be satisfied with the kitchen." Before Vi could speak, he grabbed her arm and began to pull her through the crowd. He stopped at one table, then another—each time shaking his head and saying, "Not here."

When they reached the far end of the room, Vi was convinced that she had been overlooked, and she felt tears coming to her eyes. "They can squeeze me in at Mamma's table," she said plaintively, just as Ed drew her up before their grandfather.

Horace was standing in front of the large table. "Miss Violet Adelaide Travilla," he said, bending slightly forward and extending his arm to her. "Will you allow me the great pleasure of escorting you to your place of honor?"

Vi placed her hand on his arm, and all of a sudden, she was aware that the voices of all the guests were stilled. Horace led her to an empty chair next to Wealthy, and as she took her seat, he said, "Happy birthday, darling." And another cheer went up in the room.

Flushing with pleasure, and some embarrassment, Vi whispered to her aunt, "I thought I'd have to eat in the kitchen."

"Oh, no, Cinderella," Wealthy said. "Tonight, you are the belle of the ball."

Horace had seated himself at Vi's other side, and the rest of the guests soon settled at their tables throughout the room. Vi turned to her grandfather and said, "Thank you for this surprise, Grandpapa."

"Do not credit me, my dear, for it was Wealthy who determined the seating and your mother, grandmother, and Aunt Lottie who devised the ruse to get you to the head table. I am but a mere actor in their play, and I was not told of my role until just minutes ago. I fear the ladies do not trust me with their secrets."

"We trust you completely, Horace, to hold your tongue," Wealthy interjected. "We were simply afraid that you might give us away with your face. You were never adept at hiding your feelings for long." To Vi, Wealthy remarked, "I hope you do not mind dining with all us old folks. Our talk will probably be as musty as the cottage before you cleaned it."

"But I couldn't be happier," Vi said gaily.

Before the dinner began, Reverend Cyril Keith stood and offered a prayer. Then Harry Duncan (who was Wealthy's nephew, raised by her after his parents died) officially welcomed all the family and special guests to the celebration of Wealthy's one-hundredth year and the reuniting of so many descendants of the Stanhope family. It was a charming speech and included a special recognition for Vi, who was, Harry noted, the only one of the family to share the birth month of June with Aunt Wealthy. Then Mayor Castle rose and extended his welcome — "as the democratically elected representative of all Lansdalians." The mayor was both gracious and unusually brief, and then dinner was served.

Vi enjoyed the excellent meal and spoke politely whenever she was spoken to, but mostly she enjoyed listening to the conversations around her. Aunt Wealthy and Vi's great-grandfather spent much of the meal reminiscing about the days before anyone else in the room had been born, and Vi heard the name "Eva" mentioned many times in the sweetest of tones. To her other side, Horace and Marcia Keith were also discussing years long since past, including the time that Horace visited his cousin and her young family in Pleasant Plains. Vi realized that such discussions were taking place at all the tables in the room, and she wished there were some way she could hear every one of them, for these people — her family — were part of her own history.

When all that was left to be served was dessert, Vi wondered if there might be dancing later. Just as she had that thought, she heard a commotion of some sort at the side of the room. Men were entering, and she recognized Mr. Montgomery and his sons. *So there will be music*, she thought. As the band quickly assembled, the guests hushed their conversations in anticipation.

At the far end of the table, Stuart Keith rose. "It is customary to conclude so fine a meal with dessert," he began, "but we will break with custom a bit tonight. Many years ago, when I married into the Stanhope family, I quickly learned to enjoy unpredictability." Knowing laughter came from many parts of the room.

"So if you can wait for your sweets," Stuart continued, "there are some here who have words for our Wealthy. I will begin with the word 'extraordinary,' for Wealthy, you are an extraordinary person. All about you tonight are people whom you have touched and influenced. From your example, many of us here have learned to see the extraordinary possibilities in each day God gives us. You have always demanded the best of yourself. You've never been afraid to defy conventional thinking and to take on seemingly impossible tasks."

Stuart continued in this vein for another minute or so, then introduced his son Rupert, who took the word "courage" as the theme of his salute. Harry Duncan spoke next on the word "selflessness," and he was followed by Dr. King, whose theme was "friendship." The final tribute belonged to Horace, and he gave brief but eloquent remarks on "forgiveness."

Then Stuart Keith stood once more and said, "Our final word for you tonight is "endurance."

Wealthy threw her small hands into the air and laughed. "You've had many generous words for me," she said, "but at last—one that really suits. Whatever else I may have done in my life, I can rightly lay claim to endurance. And I cannot *endure* waiting any longer for my dessert."

The whole room broke into an uproar of laughing and clapping. Stuart, who had expected some comment of this kind from Wealthy, could barely stifle his own amusement. But in a booming voice, he declared, "Your wish is our command, Aunt Wealthy. Bring on the cake!"

At his signal, the gaslights in the ballroom were dimmed, and two waiters suddenly appeared, carrying a large silver tray on which an enormous cake, frosted in white, towered. Its six layers had been decorated with flags painted in red and blue frosting—each one representing a flag that had flown over the United States since the day of Wealthy's birth. Atop the cake, instead of candles, lighted sparklers flashed and glittered like dancing comets, and the dazzling sight drew applause from everyone.

The waiters very carefully set the tray on the table, and as if by a magician's trick, Wealthy disappeared from view—hidden behind her birthday cake. Realizing that they had just obscured the guest of honor, the waiters slid the cake to the side, and the tiny little woman reappeared, her face beaming almost as brightly as the sparklers.

Everyone rose to their feet and clapped. The band began to play, and a solo voice as pure and strong as a mountain stream sang:

> Should auld acquaintance be forgot,
> And never brought to mind?
> Should auld acquaintance be forgot,
> And auld lang syne!

Throughout the room, the descendants of the Stanhope family joined hands, and every voice was raised in the familiar chorus. Mrs. O'Flaherty then sang the second and third verses of the song, and the guests followed her in a final round of the chorus. Instantly, the band struck another chord, and the young men of Wealthy's family started singing, "For she's a jolly good fellow!"

Meanwhile, the waiters were busily cutting the cake and distributing plates to all the tables. As the guests started to eat, Wealthy tugged at Vi's sleeve and said in a low voice, "Do you think I should make a speech? So many kind things have been said about me, but I am terrified of speaking to groups, though they be my kith and kin. Always have been. I would hate to spoil this wonderful evening by keeling over in a faint."

Vi smiled and said, "I think you should do what is right for you, Aunt Wealthy. There's no need for a speech if you don't want to make one."

With a sigh of relief, Wealthy said, "Oh, good! Do you think they have more planned for us?"

Vi replied, "I believe there may be dancing."

94

"That would be very pleasant," Wealthy said. "I always enjoy watching others dance, and no one expects a woman of my age to take the floor." She leaned closer to Vi and whispered, "I have two left feet, you know, and in my youth, I caused many young gentlemen a great deal of pain. I used to say that I would marry the first man I met with two *right* feet. Of course, two right feet means no wrong feet, so I never met that man."

Vi giggled and said, "I am not very good at dancing myself, Aunt Wealthy, though I'm learning."

A few moments later, Horace rose and went to Aunt Wealthy's side. Bending near his aunt's ear, he whispered something that Vi could not hear. Wealthy nodded, and then Horace stood at his full height and called for the attention of the guests.

"I have requested a dance with my aunt," he said, "and she has most politely but firmly refused me. But I am determined to have the first waltz, and so I would like to ask my lovely granddaughter to be my partner."

Despite her uncertainty about her skills, Vi stood and took Horace's hand and let him guide her to the space in front of the main table. The band began to play one of the most popular of Strauss's Viennese waltzes, and Horace led Vi around the floor. Vi had learned to count the moves in her mind—one, two, three, one, two, three—but her grandfather was so sure of step that she forgot to count and found herself gliding with ease. *It's almost like flying*, she thought. Catching Horace's reassuring smile, she knew that she was doing it correctly.

As the dance progressed, she became aware that others had come to the floor. She saw her cousin Millie and Dr. Landreth glide by, and Harry and May Duncan, and Trip and Eloise Dinsmore and then Isa and Cousin James! She was most surprised when Horace stopped though the music played on. But with a bow, Horace thanked her and excused himself, and Ed took her waist and continued the dance.

"You've been taking lessons," Ed commented. "And they must be working."

"Is that a compliment?" Vi asked.

"Indeed it is, for you are as graceful as any young lady with whom I have ever waltzed."

"Don't tease me, big brother."

"I'm not. Really, Vi, you dance beautifully. If my compliment was not gracious, it's just because I'm not used to thinking of my pesky little sister as a beautiful young lady who will soon be twirling around ballrooms and breaking the hearts of all the young men."

Vi flushed and said, "I have no wish to break hearts, but I think I shall always love to dance. I imagine that this is how it feels to fly."

The music ended, and Vi suggested that Ed take her place at the table so that he might chat with Aunt Wealthy and their Great-Grandpa. She went to find her mother's table. As she made her way across the ballroom, Vi was often stopped to receive good wishes on her birthday. When she reached the table, only Missy and the twins were still seated.

Herbert pointed and said, "Mamma's way over there with Aunt Louise. They're talking with Cousin James's father and the Osbournes."

"And Isa's dancing with Cousin James again," Harold added, a hint of disapproval in his voice. "Do you think they *like* each other or something?"

"I know they like each other," Vi said, "for we all like each other."

Harold was clearly not satisfied with Vi's response, but Herbert grabbed him by the shoulder and said, "Let's go watch the band. Mamma said that they're going to play some country dances and one of the musicians plays spoons!"

Music from spoons being much more interesting than more talk of Isa and Cousin James, Harold and Herbert were off to see the band—leaving Vi and Missy alone.

"So, what is happening with Isa?" Vi asked her sister.

"Love," Missy said softly. "It was obvious the minute James arrived at Ion for the trip here. The first thing he did was ride off to Roselands. He said he wanted to see Great-Grandpa, but we all knew who was really in his thoughts. It's as plain as day that he adores Isa, and she him."

"And?" Vi asked, for she knew there was more to the story.

Missy lowered her voice. "And the only problem is—well, you can guess."

"Aunt Louise," Vi said flatly.

"She's always wanted Isa and Virginia to marry wealthy husbands," Missy went on. "She's afraid that her daughters might be forced into poverty just as she was after Mr. Conley was killed in the war. But Aunt Louise just doesn't understand that true wealth cannot be measured in coins. Cousin James is a pastor, and he'll never be rich in money. And Aunt Louise simply won't see how rich he is in spirit."

"Has she refused to let Isa marry him?" Vi asked.

"Not exactly, for Great-Grandpa is all in favor of the match. And I'm sure that Aunt Louise really does like Cousin James. She hasn't said 'no,' but she hasn't said 'yes,' either. Isa is doing everything she can to win her mother's consent. And James, too. But it is so frustrating. Aunt Louise keeps talking about Virginia and her rich husband and what a grand life they are living in New York. Aunt Louise hasn't even seen Virginia since the wedding last fall, and still she almost taunts Isa with stories about Virginia's 'important social position' and her 'elegant New York townhouse' and her 'lavish entertaining.' "

"Isa doesn't care about things like that," Vi huffed.

"No, she never has," Missy agreed. "But Aunt Louise keeps comparing her to Virginia, and poor Isa must summon every ounce of her strength to stay calm. She jokes that between them, she and James are taking up every second of the Lord's time with their prayers. But they both trust Him completely to guide them through this."

"Can't anybody do anything to convince Aunt Louise?" Vi wondered.

"Mamma is trying," Missy said. "She and Grandpapa arranged for Aunt Louise and Isa to come to the reunion so they could meet James's family and Aunt Louise could see for herself what good people they are. James's father has been very kind to Aunt Louise since we arrived, and James himself treats her with great respect and deference. We are all praying for them."

"Even for Aunt Louise?" Vi asked.

"Oh, especially for Aunt Louise," Missy asserted. "Her life has been so sad, and yet she has never been willing to open her heart to the One who can truly ease her pain and comfort her in sorrow. She's really not a bad person, you know, but she has cut herself off from God's love and can only wander in the wilderness she has made for herself."

"I'll pray for them, too," Vi promised. *And most of all for Aunt Louise*, she told herself, *because she needs You so much, Lord*.

Vi was suddenly shaken from her thoughts by a soft hand on her shoulder. She looked up into the smiling face of Millie Keith Landreth. Instantly Vi and Missy stood to greet their cousin.

"Please be seated, girls," Millie said, "and I will join you for a few minutes. I'm not used to so much dancing, and I have begged to be excused from the next set."

At that moment, Ed rushed up to the table. He greeted Millie, then turned to Missy and said, "Big sister, you have to be my dance partner. It's a quadrille. Vi, do you want a partner?"

"No, I don't know the steps," Vi said firmly. "But thanks anyway."

"It's your party, so I won't argue," Ed smiled. He grabbed his older sister's hand, and they hurried away to join the couples on the dance floor.

"I'm glad to have a few minutes with you, Vi," Millie said, "to wish you a happy birthday and to tell you how much this reunion means to all of us. You cannot know how delighted I am to see your grandparents and your mother. The last time I saw Elsie, she was no taller than this table. And now she is grown and has all you fine children."

"But I didn't know that you and Mamma ever met before," Vi said in surprise.

Millie laughed and said, "She did not know either. At least she didn't remember. But yes, I was visiting at Roselands many years ago and accompanied your great-grandfather when he went to get Elsie in Louisiana. It was quite an adventure for me, though it was hard for your mother. She was barely four years old and leaving the only home she'd ever known. It's no wonder that she has forgotten. More than forty years have passed, and I just thank our dear Lord that He has brought us together again. I hope He will give us more opportunities to be together, for family is one of the greatest blessings He bestows on us."

"Oh, yes, ma'am, it is," Vi agreed.

"I have waited so long for this reunion," Millie said, a faraway look coming to her eyes, "and it's been a hard wait, though I always trusted that God would lead us to this day in His time. Truly, Vi, I can hardly express my happiness at seeing your great-grandfather, your grandfather, and your mother. And meeting all my young cousins. . ."

"I would like to know you better," she said with a warm smile, "for Aunt Wealthy tells me that you are a most interesting young lady."

Vi felt herself flush as she replied, "That was kind of her to say. But you and Dr. Landreth—what fascinating lives you live. I was hoping that I might have a chance to ask you about your missionary service, Mrs. Landreth."

"I will be glad to share our stories with you," Millie said. "But only if you promise to call me Cousin Millie. Will you do that?"

"Yes, ma'am," Vi said happily. Then she added, "Yes, Cousin Millie."

"Then we should make an appointment," Millie said with a charming briskness. "I would like to ask you and your elder sister and brother to lunch with the Landreths on Monday. I've discussed it with Elsie, and she will come too. Charles and I thought we might all dine here at the hotel. My daughter Fanny will join us and perhaps the others. Will you come?"

100

"Oh, yes!" Vi exclaimed, her eyes sparkling with pleasure at this unexpected invitation. "Thank you very much."

"Good, and look—your sister and brother are finished with their dance," Millie said. "I can ask them as well."

She reached over and took Vi's hand, squeezing it lightly. "You know, Vi, that I am a grandmother. And yet tonight I feel quite like a girl."

Vi looked closely at her cousin. Millie's hair was gray, the kind of pale, golden gray that is the heritage of blondness. Her face was lined, and there were crinkles at the corners of her eyes that reminded Vi of Mrs. O'Flaherty. Vi guessed that Millie must be in her late fifties, and yet she saw the girl in the lift of Millie's mouth as she smiled and the clear blue of her bright eyes.

"And I feel a bit more grown up," Vi replied just as Missy and Ed reached the table.

The party went on into the night, though Aunt Wealthy and old Mr. Dinsmore both left before nine o'clock. The dancing was a great success, and Mrs. O'Flaherty entertained again with a program of Irish folk songs. Then the guests began to drift away. Most rode in carriages, but Vi, Katie, Missy, and Ed chose to walk and enjoy the soft, warm night.

By eleven, only the Allisons, Horace and Rose, and Elsie remained. Lottie and Richard excused themselves to meet briefly with the hotel manager, so the others gratefully sank down on a comfortable couch in the hotel lobby. Elsie and Rose were discussing the party when Horace suddenly remembered the letter in his pocket. *No time like the present*, he thought, and he started to read.

He read the letter once, then a second time. By now, both his wife and daughter had noticed his worried expression.

"Is it bad news, dear?" Rose asked.

He looked up and nodded. Then he handed the letter to Elsie, saying, "It is from my old friend Mitchell Love."

Elsie knew the name. She took the sheets, and as she read the words, her face drained of color. She looked up, her eyes dark with fear. "What are we to do, Papa?" she pleaded. "However can I tell her?"

CHAPTER

8

An Early Departure

When you pass through the waters, I will be with you. . . .

ISAIAH 43:2

An Early Departure

*E*lsie was up early the next morning. She dressed quickly, and stopping only to tell Phyllis that she would not return until lunchtime, Elsie walked directly to the Allisons' house. Lottie and Richard were having coffee with Rose and Horace in a bright sunroom at the rear of the house.

"Is she awake yet?" Elsie asked.

"I heard stirring in her room, so I think she will be down soon," Lottie said.

"I thought and prayed a great deal last night," Elsie said, taking a seat next to Lottie. "I don't want this to interfere with the reunion, but I must tell the children what has happened. Papa and I can explain to Aunt Wealthy and Grandpa and Aunt Marcia and Uncle Stuart. I don't want to be false with anyone, but I think we should phrase it in the best light."

"Yes, I agree," Horace said. "There is no reason to frighten anyone before we know exactly what the real situation is."

"Are you sure you do not want to make the trip, dearest?" Rose asked Elsie.

"I want to, and I debated much during the night," Elsie replied. "But I know that Papa is the best one to go. The other children need me, for this will be terrifying for them." She nearly choked with emotion as she added, "It is just too soon for them. Edward's death is still too fresh for them to face. . ."

Lottie's arm was around her shoulders, holding her close. "I think you are absolutely right to stay," Lottie said in a tone at once warm and firm. "We must all pray that the outcome of Horace's journey is positive, but if that is not God's will, then all your children will need you, Elsie, your youngest no less than your eldest."

The adults continued to talk until some minutes later, a light tapping was heard at the sunroom door and Missy entered. She was dressed in a pale green summer frock, and her brown hair, worn high off her slim neck, seemed highlighted with gold as the sunlight touched it.

To Elsie, her eldest daughter looked as beautiful and innocent of care as the first day of summer. *Dear Lord, give me strength*, Elsie prayed silently. *Strength enough to sustain her through this day and whatever the coming days may hold for her.*

Missy had seen immediately that her elders were discussing something serious. "Should I come back later?" she asked.

"No, dear," Elsie said. "Come sit here with me."

As Missy went to the couch, Lottie and Richard excused themselves, saying that they had some household duties to attend to.

Elsie took her daughter's hands and looked into her eyes. "We have something to tell you, and it will not be easy. But God is with you and with all whom you love."

Missy could not imagine what her mother was going to say, but she knew that she had not seen such pain in Elsie's eyes since the day of Edward Travilla's fatal accident. Quite beyond her control, the girl's hands began to tremble.

"Has someone died?" she asked fearfully.

"Oh, no," Elsie said. "But your grandfather has received word from a friend, and. . ." Her voice failed her, and she looked to Horace.

"It's Lester, dear," Horace said. "My friend, Mr. Love, has written from Rome that Lester is ill."

Missy could not take in the words.

"Lester is very ill," Elsie said, her voice now unwavering. "He apparently contracted a fever while on an excursion to one of the southern Italian regions. He returned to Rome and managed to contact Mr. Love. Lester is under a doctor's care, and Mr. Love tells us that this physician is excellent. But Lester has not recovered as expected, and Mr. Love has written that his condition is serious."

Missy bit her lip to stop the tears that threatened. When she spoke, her voice was clear. "I must go to him," she said. "He needs me, and I must go."

"And you shall," Horace said. "We are already making the arrangements. The first train to the East leaves here tomorrow morning, and I have telegraphed my agent in New York to reserve us places on the next ship that departs for Europe."

"You—you will go with me, Grandpapa?" Missy said.

"Of course, I will."

"And you, Mamma?"

Elsie put an arm around Missy's shoulder and drew her close. "I want to, but I believe that your grandfather is better suited to accompany you."

"You and Horace may be in Rome for some time," Rose said. "It sounds as though Lester's recuperation may be slow and he will need tender nursing, possibly for weeks. Your mother is also needed here for your brothers and sisters. You have all suffered so much, and we all agree that the younger children should not be left for a long period."

"Recuperation," Missy said hopefully. "Then Lester is not dying."

Horace, choosing his words with great care, replied, "Not that we know. But Mr. Love writes that the fever is persistent. It comes and goes, and each bout of it has weakened Lester. Dear Missy, you must understand that Lester is still in danger, perhaps grave danger. You will need all your faith and courage for this journey."

Finally, Missy's tears did flow, and she grasped her mother and wept. "He needs me," she sobbed. "Oh, why is he so far away? Why has this happened to him?"

Elsie had no answers, so she cradled her child, kissing her forehead and rocking her gently as she had so often when Missy was a little girl. Gradually the tide of Missy's grief began to ebb, and she asked her mother for a handkerchief to dry her tears.

"There, I am done," Missy said at last. "Tears will do little good for Lester. I have to be strong, Mamma, if I am to help him."

"We will all be strong for you and for him," Elsie said. "You must not try to carry this burden alone. Never forget that you and Lester have a Friend always, and His unfailing love is your comfort. God is with you and Lester, and He will give you strength to endure whatever may come."

Rose went to sit beside Missy. "Do not dismiss your tears either," she said softly. "As our Heavenly Father has told us, 'There is a time for everything, and a season for every activity under heaven.... a time to weep and a time to laugh....' Even our Lord wept for a loved one, so follow His model." Looking at her husband, Rose added, "I can assure you that your Grandpapa has a ready shoulder for you to cry on when you have need."

Missy smiled—a little smile but one that seemed to brighten the entire room. "Thank you," she said. "Thank you all so much for being with me."

An Early Departure

They talked more, and some minutes later, Lottie and Richard rejoined them. It was decided that the Dinsmores should attend church that morning with the Allisons and the Keiths, but that Elsie would stay with Missy and begin the packing. Fortunately, as it was Sunday, no special events had been planned and the reunion guests would all be dining with their various hosts or at the hotel. Missy and Elsie's absence from these gatherings was unlikely to be noticed.

It was a while later, as they were sorting through Missy's clothing, that Elsie raised another idea she had had during her sleepless night.

"I believe that you and Papa may need companions on your trip," Elsie said. "You and he will be devoting your time to Lester, yet there are other things to be done. So I was thinking that Violet and Mrs. O'Flaherty might join you. What do you think, dear?"

"But would Vi want to come?" Missy responded. "I would love to have her with me, but it might mean that she must give up all her summer plans."

"I believe that she would rather be at your side," Elsie said. "I considered sending Ed, but he has a full summer of classes scheduled. Then I thought of Vi. Mrs. O'Flaherty has spoken to me of how helpful Vi has been to your Aunt Wealthy this last month and how well your sister adapted to the way life is lived in Lansdale. I think she can be of real value to you and your grandfather. We have seen that Mrs. O'Flaherty can handle anything that comes her way. She is also comfortable in Europe, for I believe that she lived in Rome for several years. But this must be your decision."

Missy needed no time to consider. "I would be endlessly grateful for their company, Mamma, but the decision is really for Vi and Mrs. O'Flaherty to make."

109

"Then I have your permission to speak to them?" Elsie asked.

"Oh, yes," Missy agreed.

When the Dinsmores returned from church, Elsie left Missy in Rose's care. Then she and Horace went straight to Wealthy's house. The Travilla children were all wondering why their mother had not attended services that morning, so Elsie took them out to the garden and made known the difficult news of Lester's illness and Missy's planned departure for Italy. Horace, meanwhile, discussed the situation with Wealthy and Mrs. O'Flaherty.

Elsie was careful not to alarm her children, and the younger ones were quick to accept her explanation that Lester Leland was ill and that Missy and Grandpapa were going to Rome to help him recover. But they were naturally worried about their big sister. Rosemary in particular was not easily convinced that Missy should make a voyage across the Atlantic. Elsie was very gentle and offered assurances that Grandpapa was an experienced traveler.

Rosemary finally said, "I guess it's okay as long as Grandpapa is going."

"And God," Danny declared. "God is going with them."

Elsie smiled at her young son and said, "That's right, Danny. God is with us everywhere, and with Him, we never have to be afraid. I think we should ask Him right now to guide and protect our Missy and Grandpapa."

"And to make Lester feel good real fast," Danny added.

So Elsie led them in a prayer for the travelers and for Lester. When Phyllis called them to lunch a few minutes later, Elsie excused her younger children but asked Vi and Ed to stay. Quickly, she told them all that she knew of Lester's condition and the care he was receiving; then she made her proposal that Vi join the little travel party.

Vi accepted without hesitation, and even the reminder that she might miss the family's trip to Viamede later in the summer did not dissuade her. Ed, too, was anxious to accompany his sisters and grandfather, but Elsie made it clear that he should not interrupt his studies. "I know how you feel, Ed dear, for I want more than anything to be with Missy when the ship sails," she said. "But you and I have other responsibilities, and we must make decisions with our heads as well as our hearts. Many times last night, as I pondered what course to take, I asked myself what your father would advise. And I am sure he would approve of our plans. You go back to school, and if you are needed in Italy, your Grandpapa has said that he will summon you immediately. Hopefully, they will find Lester much improved when they reach Rome."

Reluctantly, Ed agreed.

Then Vi voiced her own worry: "Are you sure I can be of help, Mamma?"

Elsie reached out and cupped her daughter's chin in her hand. "Missy needs your company and your support, dearest," she said softly. "And I am depending on you to keep your brother and me informed of how Lester is progressing. Missy and your Grandpapa will be far too busy to correspond, so you must be our eyes and ears in Rome. And you won't be alone. We are asking Mrs. O'Flaherty to make the trip as well. Your Grandpapa is speaking with her and Aunt Wealthy. Let's go in now and tell the others that you, too, will be leaving Lansdale. Then we will pack your bags."

Elsie took both her children's hands, and they were walking to the house when Vi remembered something important. "Our luncheon tomorrow with Cousin Millie and her family!" she exclaimed. "I must tell her that I can't attend."

"I will give Millie your regrets, and Missy's," Elsie assured.

Meanwhile, Mrs. O'Flaherty had gladly agreed to make the journey. In her conversation with Horace, she revealed another of her many talents—fluency in the Italian language. Horace inquired aloud if there was no end to Mrs. O'Flaherty's abilities, but Wealthy warned him "not to look a *horse gift* in the mouth." The elderly lady went on, "It is not coincidence that brought Mrs. O'Flaherty to Lansdale. I have lived long enough never to question anything, for every wonder on earth is part of our Heavenly Father's plan. Remember the words of Jonah when he was in the belly of the great fish: 'In my distress I called to the LORD, and he answered me.' Even in the darkest hours of distress, you need only call Him, and He will always provide."

When Horace left Wealthy's house a short while later, he went straight to the Lansdale Hotel to inform his father and Trip of the change in plans. Old Mr. Dinsmore was greatly disturbed by the news of Lester's illness, but he and Trip both agreed that Missy should go to her fiancé and that Horace was the best person to accompany her.

There was, however, one voice of dissent. Louise Conley, who had been included in the discussion, made it plain what she thought of the whole venture. "To drag those two girls across the ocean when Mr. Leland may be dead and in his grave at this moment — why, it is outrageous. Who will guard Violet when you and Missy are occupied?"

Horace, containing his temper, replied that Mrs. O'Flaherty was also making the journey.

Louise threw up her hands in horror and exclaimed, "That woman! Why, she is no fit chaperone. You know nothing of her past, Horace. From what I have seen, this Mrs. O'Flaherty seems more suited to a music hall stage."

"Bah!" old Mr. Dinsmore exploded. "Louise, I will thank you to still your mouth. Horace and Elsie are doing what is right for Missy, and your approval is not required."

Louise bristled at the rebuke, but she knew enough not to argue further.

"Go with our blessings and prayers, my boy," Mr. Dinsmore said in softer tones. "Do whatever you must to save that boy and secure our Missy's happiness. And Horace, you take good care of our Vi," Mr. Dinsmore added, his voice gruff with emotion. "She's strong and smart, but she's also inexperienced. Louise was right about one thing — Vi should not be left on her own in a city like Rome. Be sure our Vi understands that."

Horace went to his father's chair and bent to hug him. "I will, Papa," he said. "I will keep her safe."

"God go with you, my son," the old man said.

Then Horace offered his hand to Louise. She took it, saying "Good fortune to you" in a stiff tone that betrayed her simmering anger.

Horace and Trip left their father's bedroom, but as they stood in the sitting room, they heard the old man's voice through the door: "Now, don't you be gossiping about this to anyone, Louise. Not one word about music halls and such nonsense. You're a grown woman, and it's about time you stopped being the fly in everyone's ointment."

Horace and Trip turned to leave before they heard Louise's response. But father and son were both smiling when they reached the hotel lobby.

"There's no one quite like Grandpa, is there?" Trip said.

His expression turning serious, Horace grasped his son's arm. "Watch your grandfather carefully, Trip. For all his spunk, he is not strong. Louise may be maddening, but she is very good to him, so stay in close touch with her. And help your Mamma. Rose is so good to others that she often forgets to be good to herself."

Laying his hand over his father's, Trip said, "Don't worry, Papa. You must concentrate on what is most important now. You have our love, and God is with you all. May He grant you a safe voyage and return Lester to us in good health."

After one final embrace, Horace forced himself to leave. He decided to walk back to the Allisons' house, for he needed time to think. He had taken many long journeys in his life. He had traveled the world and lived for years on foreign shores. But never before had he felt such a sense of urgency and, he had to admit to himself, foreboding before a voyage.

Horace had not shown Missy the letter from Mr. Love, for his friend had written too plainly. Lester Leland had been near death more than once, and only the young man's strong constitution and will to live had pulled him back from the brink. But each new bout of fever was sapping Lester's strength, and Mr. Love feared that willpower would not be sufficient to save him.

We are in Your hands, dear Father in Heaven, Horace prayed, *and we draw our strength from You. Please, Lord, fortify me for*

An Early Departure

Missy and Lester's sake, and grant me the humility to accept whatever may be the outcome of our journey. Please strengthen that boy so that he may defeat this illness and rise again from his bed of pain. But if it is Your will to take him now, then receive him into Your Kingdom of love.

As Horace prayed, a passage from Hebrews came suddenly to his mind: "We have this hope as an anchor for the soul, firm and secure. It enters the inner sanctuary behind the curtain, where Jesus, who went before us, has entered on our behalf."

Horace knew in his heart that God had answered his prayer. He quickened his step. *Thank You, Lord,* he thought as the Allison home came into view. *Thank You for reminding me of Your great message of hope. The journey ahead of us may be difficult, but we are never helpless with You as our anchor.*

CHAPTER

9

The Journey

*I waited patiently for the LORD;
he turned to me and heard
my cry.*

PSALM 40:1

The Journey

From Vi's journal, dated Wednesday, June 18, 1879:

Tomorrow morning the ship arrives in France, and Grandpapa says we should be in Rome by dawn of the next day. We are all trying to keep Missy's spirits up, though nothing but the sight of Lester will relieve her fears. I wish there were something more I could do for her. Grandpapa and Mrs. O'Flaherty have both reminded me how Paul prayed for the Colossians, that they might have "great endurance and patience." But it is so hard to be patient when we don't know what is happening. Grandpapa has written to Mr. Love, and we are hoping to receive more word of Lester when we land in France. Missy is so brave. She doesn't complain, and she doesn't cry when we are with her. But I've seen her eyes, and I know she sheds tears when she is alone. Grandpapa has tried to get her to participate in some of the activities on the ship, but she prefers to stay in her room and to have her meals there. Grandpapa has agreed, though he insists that for her health, she take walks on the deck several times each day. Mrs. O'Flaherty joins her for meals to encourage her to eat.

Oh, yes. I had a birthday party, though it's been several days since I actually turned sixteen. Grandpapa must have talked to the Captain, because we sat at his dinner table tonight, and he had a beautiful cake, with candles, served. The band played, and everybody clapped when I cut the cake. It was such a surprise and so nice that, for a few minutes, I forgot why we are all on this ship. When I told Grandpapa later, he hugged me and said that I shouldn't feel guilty about forgetting. Grandpapa said that God helps us through the hardest of times, and sometimes that means we are able to put our troubles aside for a while and enjoy ourselves and renew our energy for what lies ahead. Grandpapa said, "God shows us His mercy in many ways, and there are times when we may not even realize that His hand is guiding us." I took a piece of birthday cake to Missy after dinner, and I told her what Grandpapa and I had talked about. She said that she hadn't considered his point before, but she thought he was right, that God helps us be strong in crisis in ways that we cannot comprehend. Then she gave me the best birthday present ever, though she didn't know it. She ate every bit of the cake!

The great ship reached port on schedule the next day, and a letter from Mr. Love was waiting in the office of the ship company. The news, which was several days old, was not good. Lester had suffered another relapse, and the new bout of fever had weakened him more. Mr. Love also stated that he had booked rooms for the travelers at the Hotel Roma and that he would be there to meet them. Horace immediately dispatched a telegram to Mr. Love, informing him of their expected arrival time.

Missy took the news of Lester's relapse with outward calm, and Vi again marveled at her sister's courage. *She is so like Mamma,* Vi thought. *I know that she is terrified for Lester, yet she doesn't panic or cry. How can she be so strong? But I know the answer to that already. Missy walks with You, Lord, and You are her strength.*

The Journey

The train trip to Rome seemed swifter than Vi, who was used to the great distances of her native country, expected. Even Missy was captivated by the French towns and countryside that passed their window. But at dinner that evening, Missy grew silent and distracted, and she barely noticed when anyone spoke to her. Returning to the compartment which the ladies shared, Mrs. O'Flaherty tried to lighten the mood with stories of her years in Rome. Horace joined the little party just as Mrs. O'Flaherty was explaining why she and her husband had moved there several years after their marriage.

"Mr. O'Flaherty became ill while we were living in Paris. It was a particularly damp and cold autumn, and although Ian improved, his strength was slow to return. So his doctor advised us to go south to a warmer climate. I had fantasies of living on the southern coast of France, but that was not possible," Mrs. O'Flaherty recalled. "We had to support ourselves and pay for Ian's medical bills. Our best hope, it seemed, was a large city full of families with daughters and sons who required education in the musical arts. In Paris, I had begun to tutor in piano and singing, and Ian was also teaching, though his main occupation was composing. Fortunately, our Parisian employers provided us with excellent references, so I was able to secure work almost as soon as we arrived in Rome. Ian was still recuperating, but Rome was a tonic for him."

"Did you mind leaving Paris?" Vi asked.

"Not at all, though I do believe that Paris is the most beautiful city in all Europe. But I could have been happy anywhere so long as I was with my husband. And Rome agreed with us both. What a place for artists! Such grandeur and such history—but you will soon see for yourselves."

"I hope so," Missy said in a small voice.

"Have confidence, my girl," Mrs. O'Flaherty replied. She added with emphasis, "*When* Mr. Leland has recovered, he will show you all the splendors of Rome."

"But what if he doesn't recover?" Missy suddenly demanded. And for the first time since they had left Lansdale, the others saw tears rolling from her beautiful eyes.

"Then you will bear it," Mrs. O'Flaherty said softly. "But now is not the time to give way to fear and doubt. Mr. Leland will need your confidence and hope to strengthen his own."

"Mrs. O'Flaherty is right, dearest," Horace said. "The future is beyond our control, so we must focus on the present and what we can all do to help Lester make a full recovery. I know that you will fight for him, but you must understand what your chief weapon will be — the power of your loving prayers for Lester and your faith in God's love for him. Doubt is the enemy of faith."

Vi, who was sitting beside her sister in the comfortable train compartment, seized Missy's hand and said, "Oh, you must not be fearful, Missy. Remember what Jesus told the disciples when He had withered the fig tree." Vi quoted the passage from Mark: "'Have faith in God,'" Jesus answered. "I tell you the truth, if anyone says to this mountain, "Go, throw yourself into the sea," and does not doubt in his heart but believes that what he says will happen, it will be done for him. Therefore I tell you, whatever you ask for in prayer, believe that you have received it, and it will be yours.'"

Vi, squeezing Missy's hand hard, declared with the full passion of her faith, "We are so close now, Missy, so close to Lester. And I just know that he is waiting for you to help him. With God, you can move mountains. I know you can."

Missy said nothing for several moments, but Vi saw that her tears had stopped. Then Missy smiled and said, "Thank you, darling Vi. Thank you all. You have reminded me that I only need my faith in God to move this mountain. I fear I may need such reminders often in the coming days, and I know that I can depend on you to keep my faith strong."

Horace leaned back against his seat and said, "We must strengthen one another that we may all be strong for Lester. We must ask the Lord to cleanse our hearts of doubt and fear and to fill us with hope."

"Can we pray now, Grandpapa?" Vi asked. "Will you lead us all in a prayer of hope right now?"

Horace began, and each of his companions added to the prayer. They prayed many times that night, together and in their own hearts, as the train sped through the darkness.

It was past midnight when Horace excused himself and went to his compartment. In her best practical manner, Mrs. O'Flaherty insisted that Missy lie down and sleep.

"Have we crossed the border yet?" Missy asked in a dreamy tone that conveyed her fatigue.

"Yes, girl, we have," Mrs. O'Flaherty said. "And when you awake, we shall be in Rome."

In the dark, on the seat opposite Missy, Vi moved close to Mrs. O'Flaherty and felt the good woman's arm around her shoulder. The rhythmic clacking of the train's wheels on the track and the rocking motion of the carriage lulled her, and her head drooped.

"Lay your head in my lap," Mrs. O'Flaherty said, "and try to sleep. Missy is not the only one who will need rest for the day that is coming."

Vi did as she was told, thinking that she felt as she had when she was a child, curling up in her mother's lap as the Travilla carriage wended its way back to Ion after an evening visit with her grandparents at The Oaks or her great-grandfather at Roselands. She remembered how she would wake up in her father's arms as he carried her to bed, and how he would always say, "God be with you through the night, my pet," just before she fell asleep again.

Sleep tugged at Vi's eyelids, but before she drifted off, a last small prayer formed in her mind: *We've come so far, Lord, so very far from home. Please, let the end of our journey be a new beginning for my sister and Lester. Please, Lord, restore Lester to her and to all of us. Let him live to see home again.*

Then Vi slept, and as the train plunged toward its final destination, she dreamed of Ion. In her dream, she sat beside the lake and her father was there. And they talked of hope.

CHAPTER

10

Another Reunion

I pray that you may enjoy good
health and that all may go
well with you, even as your
soul is getting along
well.

3 JOHN 2

Another Reunion

*T*he train arrived just as the sun was dawning over the ancient city, and after arranging for their luggage to be delivered, Horace and the ladies hurriedly made their way to the Hotel Roma.

As their carriage pulled to a stop before the large and elegant structure, Horace began to wave, saying, "There is our friend, Mr. Love."

Looking toward the entrance, Vi saw a man coming toward them, and she was instantly reminded of the drawings of Santa Claus that were so popular in the United States. Though Mr. Love was clad in a suit—not red and white—he sported a full white beard, and wavy puffs of white hair peeked from beneath his hat. His cheeks were round and pink. In fact, he was round all over, though not fat, and barely as tall as Vi herself.

"*Buon giorno*! Good morning and welcome to Rome," he called cheerfully. Then he turned to the driver and said something else in Italian.

Horace got down, gave the ladies his hand, and was soon introducing them to his friend.

"I have asked the driver to wait for us," Mr. Love said. "You must register, Horace, but I believe you will then want to proceed directly to Mr. Leland's apartment."

"Oh, yes," Missy exclaimed, "as quickly as possible. Does he know that we are coming?"

"He knows that you are expected, Miss Travilla," the man replied, "but I did not tell him an exact day or time. Train schedules are not always reliable, and I didn't wish to build his hopes too high."

"How is he?" Missy asked.

"When I left him last night, he seemed a little better. He has a nurse, as you know, and I alerted her that you would arrive today," Mr. Love said. "The last round of fever has left Mr. Leland very weak, but it seems to be under control, and yesterday he was able to take some nourishment. The doctor visits him morning and evening and is always on call. But now that you are here, the best medicine of all has arrived."

As they talked, Horace had gone into the hotel. Not five minutes later, he was back, and they all returned to the carriage, making room for Mr. Love. He gave directions to the driver, and they were off.

The Hotel Roma was located on a broad avenue near one of Rome's most famous plazas, and Vi had the impression of both age and luxury in the buildings they passed. But she was too attentive to the conversation between her sister, grandfather, and Mr. Love to take in more than fleeting glimpses of the scenery. Then the carriage turned off the main way, and the streets narrowed—in some places seeming hardly wide enough to accommodate their vehicle. The carriage rattled and bounced over the rough stones, but Mr. Love urged the driver to proceed as rapidly as was safe.

At last, they slowed to a halt before an unimposing stone building on a tiny street. The exterior was gray with time, and the stone steps that led up to its door had been worn down by many years of use.

"This is Mr. Leland's *pensione*," Mr. Love said as he directed them into the narrow hallway of the boarding house. "It is not much to see, but he occupies the top floor, which has a balcony and a windowed wall that makes a bright workplace for an artist. If you will follow me. . ."

They ascended the stairway, which complained in creaks and groans and pops at each step. But for all the noise, it was steady, and the group climbed quickly up the three floors to the top landing. There was a door on each side of the narrow space, and Mr. Love opened the one to the right. Missy entered first, and the sight that greeted her was just what she had expected, for Lester had described his lodgings in great detail in his letters.

The sitting room was dark but clean, with only the barest of furnishings. One wall and half of another were covered by heavy drapes from ceiling to floor, but the drapes were so old and frayed that sunlight shot through their holes and made thin shafts of light that seemed to blaze throughout the room.

A second door at the far side of the room opened and a woman in her fifties emerged. She wore a spotless white apron and a small white cap, and Vi's first impression of her was "neat as a pin."

"This is Mrs. Warden," Mr. Love said. "She has nursed Mr. Leland for weeks now, and we are very fortunate to have her."

Horace extended his hand to the woman. Hearing her greeting, he said, "You are English, Mrs. Warden?"

"Yes, sir, though many years resident here in Rome," she answered briskly. "But I can tell you of myself later." With a warm smile at Missy, she said, "I believe this young lady has someone to see now. He's awake, Miss Travilla."

Missy hurried to the door of the bedroom and laid her hand on the knob, but then she paused. "Is there anything I should know?" she asked anxiously.

"Only that the young man in there loves you more than anything on this earth," Mrs. Warden said. "He's very weak, and he's lost a good deal of weight, but I expect you can handle that. Just go in. He's been waiting a long time for the sight of you."

Missy was gone before the last words left Mrs. Warden's mouth.

As the bedroom door closed, Vi felt the sting of tears in her eyes—tears of joy for her sister. She sniffed and brushed at her cheeks, but she couldn't erase the smile that had come to her lips.

Mrs. O'Flaherty, who was standing behind her, put her strong hands on Vi's shoulders and whispered in her ear, "This is a sweet reunion, Vi girl. The good Lord is watching over those two. Watching over them as He watches over all His lambs."

Though the new arrivals all seemed rooted to the floor, Mrs. Warden did not let a minute go by. She pulled back the drapes on the large wall, and sunlight flooded the room. Then she drew aside the curtain on the smaller wall, revealing a nook that contained shelves stacked with a few plates and bowls and a great many paintbrushes in glass jars. There was also a small table atop which stood a burner and a kettle. Lighting the burner, Mrs. Warden announced that tea would soon be ready.

Her words broke the spell that seemed to have settled over everyone else, and Horace let out a loud sigh, as if he had been holding his breath for a very long time. Mr. Love rubbed his hands together and smiled gleefully, reminding Vi more than ever of Santa Claus.

"Everyone, please be seated," Mrs. Warden said. "I have English tea, if that will suit, and *biscotti* and *panini* fresh from the bakery—that's bread and buns to us English folk—and butter and cheese and some beautiful figs. So if

someone will help me, you can have your *prima colzione* —
that's breakfast — in a jiffy."

All the while she was speaking, Mrs. Warden was taking
parcels of food and a teapot and cups and saucers from
beneath the cloth skirt that covered the little table.

"I wouldn't be a bit surprised to see a white rabbit pop
out next," Mrs. O'Flaherty whispered to Vi before moving
to assist the nurse.

Suppressing a giggle, Vi went to sit on a small stool next
to the chair her grandfather had taken. Horace was looking
at his pocket watch.

"Do you realize that it is just eight o'clock? Back at The
Oaks, I would be sitting down to breakfast at this time.
Perhaps that explains why I am suddenly so ravenous. Tea
and *panini* sound like manna to me."

Soon they were all enjoying the simple but delicious
repast. As they ate, Mrs. Warden prepared a tray with two
cups and disappeared into the bedroom.

When she reappeared some minutes later, she said to
Horace, "Your granddaughter has more nursing skills than
I expected, Mr. Dinsmore."

"She has learned well from her mother," he replied. "But
tell me, Mrs. Warden, of Lester's condition."

"Doctor Di Marco can explain better than I, and he will be
here within the next half hour," she said. "I can tell you that
Mr. Leland is a good patient, sir. He knows that he is very ill,
and he does not — as some people do — attempt to do more
than he is able. Nor does he expect miracles. He is a realist.
But he is also a man of faith. He believed that he would see his
dear fiancée again, and his prayers have been answered."

"But is he still at risk?" Horace asked.

"I do not diagnose, sir," she responded a little primly. In
gentler tones, she added, "I can say that Mr. Leland is not

131

out of danger, but his fever has been near normal for twenty-four hours now and that is a good sign. He has weathered more than most. I doubt that a man less physically fit would have come this far."

Mr. Love then joined the conversation. "Mrs. Warden has much experience, Horace, and there is no better caregiver in all Rome. She trained with Miss Nightingale in London and nursed the British soldiers in the Crimea during that terrible war."

"Miss Florence Nightingale!" Vi exclaimed, her eyes sparkling with wonder. "The Lady of the Lamp!"

"Indeed, Miss Nightingale inspired me when I was just eighteen to enter nursing, and she continues to inspire me today," Mrs. Warden said.

"Have you always been a nurse, Mrs. Warden?" Vi wanted to know.

"In some form or another, Miss Violet, but hospital work is very demanding and I gave it up when I married. Then after my husband's passing, I began to do private nursing, and that is what brought me to Rome. But here now, you do not want to hear about me. Perhaps you and Mrs. O'Flaherty will help me gather the cups and plates. Dr. Di Marco will be arriving shortly, and I like to have everything clean and in its place."

Indeed, they just finished the cleaning when the creaks and groans of the hall stairs signaled the approach of the physician. He entered the apartment and was introduced by Mr. Love. Dr. Di Marco's conversation was polite — and his English nearly perfect, for he had been educated in part in England. But he excused himself quickly and went into Lester's room. A few minutes later, Missy came out.

Another Reunion

Vi had never before seen such an expression on her sister's face. Missy was almost aglow with happiness, yet at the same time, her eyes were like wells of care and pain. She closed the bedroom door and sank onto a little chair that stood beside it. Then she looked up at everyone in the room as if searching for something.

No one spoke until in a small, steady voice, Missy said, "To be with him, to hold his hand again and caress his brow, it is like a dream for me. Yet he is so very weak. Every word, every movement costs him so much effort. How can I be happy when he is still so ill? I. . . I. . . don't. . . know. . . how. . . " Her voice failed her, and she could only look from one person to the next, her eyes begging for answers.

Horace went to her, bent down on his knee, and clasped her hands. "You *do* know what to do, Missy," he said. "You cannot control Lester's destiny. That is in the hands of our Lord. But you are here for a reason—to comfort and encourage him with your love and prayers. There is no one on this earth who loves him as you do."

"I must stay with him," Missy said.

"Of course, darling," Horace assured. "We shall all stay in Rome until he is completely well."

"I mean here, in this place—*his* place," Missy said a little sharply. "I must be here day and night, at his side whenever he needs me."

"But. . ."

"I want us to be married now, Grandpapa," Missy went on. "As soon as it can be arranged. Don't you see? In my heart, Lester is my husband. He is all the world to me."

"Just as you are to him," Horace agreed.

133

"Then now is the time for us to pledge ourselves before God, to become husband and wife forever and to face whatever comes together."

Horace could see how important this decision was for Missy, but he had to raise objections—issues that he was sure she had not considered. "But what of your mother and the family? Elsie has planned—"

Missy cut off his sentence. "Mamma will understand better than anyone. She would do just the same if Papa were lying in that room. You know she would."

"Yes," Horace said slowly. "Yes, she would. And she will help the others to understand. But we must send her a message before—"

"We can't wait!" Missy cried desperately. "I will write to her immediately, but we cannot wait for her reply. Grandpapa, I know that this is right. And I think you do, too. I want to say the words, before God and man. I want to give Lester my pledge, to love him, and cherish him, and honor him 'in sickness and in health' for all the days of our lives. I cannot number our days, but however long we have, I want him to know that he will never be alone again."

Further objections were spinning in Horace's head, but he realized that none could change his granddaughter's mind. As he gazed into her eyes, he knew with certainty that she was right.

A smile appeared on his face as he said, "Does Lester agree to your proposal?"

Missy instantly wrapped her arms around her grandfather's neck. "Oh, yes, he does. He also tried to dissuade me, for my sake rather than his. But he has agreed."

"Then let me stand, my dear, and we will decide what must be done."

Missy kissed his cheek and loosed her arms. He rose and turned to his friend. "We shall need to impose on you again, Mitchell," he said to the beaming Mr. Love. "We must have a minister and a license." Then Horace turned back to his granddaughter, "But before we do this, dear, I insist that we have a long talk with Dr. Di Marco."

"Yes, yes, Grandpapa," Missy assented. "I will do whatever he says."

"Then I suggest you and I stay here and wait to speak to him," Horace said. "Mitchell, will you escort Violet and Mrs. O'Flaherty back to the hotel? I am sure our luggage has arrived there by now. I will return by lunchtime. Perhaps your daughter will also lunch with us today."

"I believe that can be arranged," Mr. Love replied with a wide grin.

As the two men discussed other plans, Vi went to Missy and slipped her arm around her sister's waist. Missy was trembling, and Vi had to ask, "Are you really sure this is what you want to do?"

"More than anything, sister, for I know that it is right for us both," Missy answered reassuringly. "Whatever the future holds, I know in my heart that our Heavenly Father wants Lester and me to be together. We will do as the doctor advises, even if he counsels delay. But I will never be separated from Lester again."

"Never?" Vi said.

Missy smiled. "I do not mean that I will never be apart from him, but when we are one in the sight of God, physical distance can never divide us. We will always be as one, though a thousand miles lie between us."

"May I still be your maid of honor?" Vi inquired.

Missy hugged her and said, "Maid of honor, cherished sister, best friend—you are all that and more. You cannot know how glad I am that you're here with me."

"I wish Mamma could be, too," Vi said as she returned her sister's embrace. "But I know she will approve of your decision. Papa would too. And Papa would be very proud of you."

So much had happened since they reached Rome that Vi felt as if she were in a daze. She was sitting with her grandfather on the balcony of their hotel suite. Missy, who had returned to the hotel after dinner, was asleep, and Mrs. O'Flaherty had gone to her room to write a letter to Mr. McFee, the manager of Viamede.

The sounds of the city drifted upward on the night air—laughter and music and the rattling of carriages and clopping of horses' hooves on the street. Looking out over the balcony, Vi saw lights everywhere. Rome, she realized, seemed to come alive at night unlike any place she had ever seen. She wondered what the people who passed below were doing. Where were they going? Her curiosity about this beautiful city, so drenched in history, came alive as it hadn't during the day when they were all so focused on Lester. A part of her wanted to rush out of the hotel and stand in the streets amidst the crowds. Yet Vi also welcomed this opportunity to be alone with her grandfather.

"What was your impression of Miss Love?" he had just inquired.

"I like her," Vi responded. "She's very pretty and as jolly as her father, I think."

"You did not find her a bit frivolous?"

136

Vi thought for a moment, then said, "No more than other girls of fourteen. She talks a lot, but I'd say that she is *enthusiastic*. At lunch today, she was very interested in hearing about the United States and told me she hopes to visit someday. It's odd to think that she is an American but has never seen her homeland."

"Zoe was born in France, when her father was serving with the American embassy there," Horace explained. "Her mother died when Zoe was quite small, and Mitchell has raised her on his own. He probably indulged her more than is good for her. They moved to Rome about three years ago, when Mitchell was assigned to the embassy here. He retired last year."

"How long has it been since you last saw Mr. Love?"

"About a dozen years, I believe. I made a trip to Paris, on business, in—let me think—in the spring of 1868. I stayed with Mitchell and his wife for two weeks. I remember that Zoe was not quite three years old, and she ruled the household, as I suspect she rules her father now. Mitchell is a fine man and an accomplished negotiator. His jovial exterior hides a sharp mind. I have seen him deal with the toughest politicians and diplomats and win their respect as well as their agreement. That is why he was so valuable to our government. If he had been willing to return to the United States, I am sure he would have risen very high, perhaps to the President's Cabinet. But with young Zoe…"

"Do you think her spoiled?" Vi asked.

"I think she lacks discipline and she asserts herself more readily than is proper for a girl of fourteen," Horace said. "But you are probably right, Vi. What a man of my years sees as a fault is probably due to her youth and not her character. I do think that her manners could use a bit of polish though. Maybe you can be a good influence on her while we are here."

Vi felt herself flush at the implied compliment, but she turned to another subject.

She had been told something of Horace and Missy's conversation with Lester's physician, but she wanted to know her grandfather's opinion. So she asked, "What did Dr. Di Marco tell you about Lester?"

"That he seems to be over the worst of it," Horace began, "and that his recuperation will be slow. As we knew, the original cause was typhus, but the doctor explained that Lester, in his weakened state, contracted a second infection and that is what has prolonged his illness. No good doctor will predict the future, but Dr. Di Marco did say that Lester's heart is sound and he has not found evidence of long-term harm to other vital organs. So he expects that with rest and care—and no further complications—Lester can recover without ill effect, though it may take some time. I must admit, however, that the doctor's quick agreement to the marriage surprised me. He said that if Lester's fever does not return in the next forty-eight hours, then the danger should be over. But his return to full strength will take weeks, perhaps months, and he will need constant attention in the beginning."

Though the darkness covered all but Vi's silhouette from him, Horace could hear a smile in her next question.

"Did he mean the attention of a wife?" she asked.

"From Mitchell's recommendation and all that I have seen today, I believe that Dr. Di Marco is a splendid physician. Very thorough and professional. But I suspect that he is also a romantic at heart. When Missy told him of her determination to marry, he agreed without a second's hesitation, requesting merely that nothing be done while Lester's condition remains in any doubt.

"Vi dear, I hope we have taught you not to put carts before horses. We must not get carried away by what we expect will occur. But our Lord and Savior has blessed us today, and for that we must be grateful. To find Lester alive and to see Missy's joy—that alone has filled my heart with hope for them."

Vi, thinking of her sister, said, "Forty-eight more hours. It isn't long, is it, Grandpapa? Yet it must seem like an eternity to Missy and Lester."

"It is less than forty hours now, dear," Horace noted. "And we will all be busy tomorrow, so the minutes will not drag for us."

"Do you think I might see Lester soon, Grandpapa? I would like him to know how happy I am for him and Missy."

"I hope so, if all goes well through this night," Horace said. "You know, dearest, that you are representing your Mamma and your brothers and Rosemary here. I was able to talk with Lester briefly today, and I did my best to assure him that the entire family will be pleased about the forthcoming marriage. There is no doubt that he wants to marry your sister, but he's worried that he may be a burden on her and on the family. He fears that his illness may do permanent damage to his health. Though Dr. Di Marco assures him it will not, Lester is having a hard time imagining himself well and fit again. He even said that Missy did not bargain on marrying an invalid and he doesn't want to hold her—and the family—to a promise made in better days. I told him that we only want what is right for Missy and that the only wrong he could do would be to deny her his love.

I'm sure he believed me, but to hear the same message from you — as a Travilla and Missy's loving and loyal sister — would mean a great deal to him."

"Do you really think so? I want to do whatever I can to help," Vi said. "But when do you think we might hear from Mamma herself?"

"Well, you know that I have sent a telegram to Ion. And Missy wrote a long letter, which we posted with the hotel manager. But there is an ocean between here and home, and I cannot guess when our communications will arrive. It could be weeks before we have your mother's response, so we must rely on our own best judgment."

"And our prayers," Vi said. "May I say my prayers with you tonight, Grandpapa?"

"I would like that very much," he said affectionately. "I think we should offer prayers of thanksgiving to our Eternal Father for bringing this reunion to pass. As we pray tonight, let us rememberHis greatest gift, Jesus, for there is no greater example of love."

CHAPTER

11

An Excellent Starting Place

*Let us do good to all people,
especially to those who
belong to the family
of believers.*

GALATIANS 6:10

*H*orace and the ladies had a brief scare the next morning. Returning to Lester's lodgings, they were informed by Mrs. Warden that her patient's fever had risen during the previous night. "But by less than two degrees," the nurse quickly added. "And it is back to normal. He breakfasted on broth and a bit of toast, and right now he's napping like a baby."

Missy, who had turned pale at the first part of this news, decided then and there that she would not leave the apartment again. Horace strongly objected to such an arrangement, but it was Mrs. Warden who proposed the solution.

"I have been occupying the rooms across the hall," she told them. "That apartment was vacant when Dr. Di Marco and Mr. Love first retained me, and Mr. Love rented it so that I could be available at all times. But as my patient is doing better, I'd planned to return to my own home as soon as Mr. Leland can manage during the night. The rooms across the hall are small, like these, but quite clean and comfortable, and there are two beds and a much better kitchen. Might not Miss Travilla take my place if she wishes to stay here through the nights?"

Horace blustered at this suggestion. "Alone! They are not married yet, Mrs. Warden. I am amazed that you would—"

The nurse cut him off instantly. "Not alone, Mr. Dinsmore. I would never suggest such a thing. My idea was that Mrs. O'Flaherty can stay with Miss Travilla. And I will come each morning and remain through the day. My little place is not far from here, so I could be summoned in a matter of minutes if

I'm needed. I understand from the doctor that you hope to move Mr. Leland soon, assuming that he continues to progress, so Miss Travilla and Mrs. O'Flaherty's stay here would be of short duration."

"Oh, that's perfect!" Missy exclaimed. "I'd feel so much better being close to Lester, and I could learn from Mrs. Warden about caring for him."

Then Mrs. O'Flaherty spoke up: "I would be happy, sir, to stay here with Missy. I have none of Mrs. Warden's skills, but I have some experience caring for the ill." A hint of amusement brightened her sapphire eyes as she added, "And I believe you know, Mr. Dinsmore, that I am an excellent chaperone of young ladies."

In the face of such arguments, Horace could not think of a reply. He cupped his chin with his hand and began to walk back and forth across the small sitting room.

Vi, having no idea what her grandfather would decide, looked questioningly to Mrs. O'Flaherty. In answer, Mrs. O'Flaherty winked, and a sly smile came to her face.

Horace continued to pace for a full minute more; then he came to a stop and looked at each of the bevy of ladies who awaited his decision.

"I surrender," he said with a sigh. "I cannot fault your logic, Mrs. Warden, nor Missy's concern for her fiancé, nor Mrs. O'Flaherty's credentials as a chaperone. You are the victors, and I am your humble servant. Just tell me what to do to make this unconventional arrangement successful."

Missy and her grandfather talked with Mrs. Warden for some time, while Mrs. O'Flaherty and Vi took their first look at the apartment across the hall. Then Horace joined them, and it was agreed that Mrs. O'Flaherty would return to the Hotel Roma to pack what she and Missy would need for the next few nights. Horace and Vi had an appointment with Mr. Love, who had arranged to help them search for new quarters for Lester.

When Lester woke, Missy and Mrs. Warden went to him, and the others prepared to leave. But as they were gathering their things, Mrs. Warden came out of the bedroom and told Vi that Lester would like to see her.

Though she had prayed for this moment, Vi suddenly felt unsure. What should she say? How could she reassure him?

Horace, who had observed the uncertainty in Vi's expression, started to say something encouraging, but he decided better. *Vi knows what to do*, he thought, *and she will do it.*

As he watched, his granddaughter drew in a deep breath and slowly exhaled. Then she squared her shoulders and erased her anxious expression with a smile. Horace was familiar with these gestures; many times, he'd watched Vi's mother do the same whenever she needed to gather her courage and face difficulty. *My dear Elsie, you've taught your daughters well*, he thought as Vi entered the bedroom. *For so many reasons, I wish you were here, but most of all to see your daughters. I shall tell you of their brave and selfless hearts and their maturity under these stressful circumstances. You will be proud, Elsie, very proud indeed.*

The window in the little bedroom was open, admitting sunlight, a warm morning breeze, and the distant sounds of the people of Rome going about their daily business. Lester lay on the plain bed, his head raised on two pillows. Missy sat beside him, holding his hand. Vi was immediately aware of how pale and thin her future brother-in-law appeared.

He looked years older than she remembered, but as she approached the bed, she saw that he, too, was smiling.

He asked her to come and sit in the empty chair opposite Missy. Though his voice was not strong, it was clear, and at the sound of it, Vi felt confidence flood through her.

"Thank you for coming to see me," Lester said as she sat down.

"Oh, I'm so glad to be here," Vi replied. "And I'm so happy for you and Missy. I know you're going to be well soon. I can see it in your eyes."

"We artists always look at the eyes first, don't we?" Lester said.

"You're the real artist, Lester," Vi said, "and I've missed your tutoring. When I am your sister-in-law, I expect you to continue my lessons."

"Missy tells me you've been a great comfort to her."

Vi glanced at Missy and said softly, "That's what sisters do."

"So what will your brothers and sister think of Missy's plan?" Lester asked. "She's bound and determined to have me as her husband. But I fear your family will be disappointed."

Vi thought for a few seconds, then responded, "Missy's right, for you two should be together. The others will be a bit jealous of me, I imagine, because I'm here with you. But they will be very happy, just as happy as I am. And Mamma, too, because she loves you so much and she wants only your happiness. Her first thought when she heard of your illness was that Missy should come to Rome and be with you."

"But I shall deprive your mother of the wedding of her firstborn," Lester noted.

"That won't matter to Mamma," Vi said firmly. "She wants what's best for Missy and you. Mamma trusts Missy and she trusts you, and she'll know that this is right. You mustn't worry, Lester."

"I trust you," he said earnestly, "to be honest with me. Do you really approve? In your heart of hearts, do you have any doubts, any worries for your sister and her future?"

"My only worry is that you are feeling needless doubt," Vi replied with feeling. "I approve. Mamma will approve. All of us approve! If Papa were alive, I know that he would approve so much that he'd be out right now, finding a minister! Lester Leland, you are just being stubborn. You love my sister and she loves you, and that's all that matters to us!"

Lester's eyes widened with wonder at Vi's short outburst, and he actually laughed, although the sound was more like a cough. Vi was afraid that she had caused him pain, but his smile widened and his face momentarily lost its worn aspect.

"Then it shall be all that matters to me," Lester said. "I should know not to argue with a Travilla female. Thank you, Vi."

He turned again to Missy, and Vi saw his hand squeeze her sister's.

"We seem to have your family's approval," he said.

Missy leaned forward and kissed him gently on the forehead. "We always have," she said in a choked voice. "So will you finally accept my proposal and be my husband?"

"With all the joy in the world, my love," he said.

The moment was so sweet, so true, that Vi hardly dared to breathe. She could not shift her eyes away from Missy and Lester, and there was no need to. She was included in the circle of their love, and her heart seemed to swell. It was all so real to her now—Lester would recover and Missy would be at his side. They would be husband and wife, and Lester would be her brother. And whatever the future held, God loved them all, and His love had banished all fear and doubt.

Vi finally rose, trying not to make a sound, and tiptoed toward the door. She was about to leave when she heard Lester's voice.

"Little sister," he said, and she instantly turned back to the bed. "You must make the most of your time here," he went on. "Rome is a treasure for one who loves beauty. I want you to visit me, but you must also make time for yourself. The museums, the churches, the Vatican, and the Roman ruins—see it all, Vi."

"But. . ." she began, ready to protest that he and Missy were her concern.

Lester lifted his hand a few inches above the sheet as if to stop her. "If I am still your teacher, little sister, then I give you this assignment, and you must complete it. See Rome and let it inspire you."

Vi couldn't help smiling. "I will, *big brother*, for I always do as my teachers say."

When Vi left her sister and Lester a few minutes later, she knew that she had done well—that she had really been of help. She'd listened to her heart, and God had given her the words. Her mother would have been more eloquent; her father would have been full of humor and common sense. But she had spoken simply, and her words had been honest, and that was all that was needed.

When her grandfather asked her how the meeting went, she thought of Psalm 121. "God helped me," she said. "He didn't let my foot slip."

An Excellent Starting Place

Horace put his arm around her shoulder and held her close. He understood exactly what she meant.

On their return to the hotel, Horace and Vi found Mr. Love and his daughter waiting for them in the luxurious lobby. Horace told Mr. Love of the new arrangements and was relieved when his friend expressed satisfaction.

"Miss Travilla should be with him, for both their sakes," the little man said. "They will strengthen one another, and Mrs. O'Flaherty will be a conscientious guardian. I am glad to know that Mr. Leland is making such progress. I had been thinking that Mrs. Warden needed some assistance. Though she is truly a Rock of Gibraltar for her patients, she requires some respite from her duties."

"Mrs. Warden will stay there tonight," Horace said. "But if all goes well and Dr. Di Marco agrees, she will move back to her home tomorrow night."

"Ah, I will organize a driver and carriage for her," Mr. Love said.

"I'm not sure what we'd have done without you, Mitchell," Horace said, placing his hand on his friend's shoulder.

"But Horace, you have done so much for me," Mr. Love protested. "Retirement does not suit me so well, you know. When you wrote that Mr. Leland would be living in Rome, I must admit that I made a project of getting to know him and assisting him in little ways when I could. I had to be most diplomatic, for he is very protective of his independence. But we became friends, and when he fell ill, he called for my help. And Horace, I felt useful again."

149

"You are always useful to me, Papa," declared young Zoe Love.

"*Merci*, my dear," Mr. Love said, "but you know what I'm talking about."

"Yes, I do. And I know you're happy, Papa, that there is more to be done for Mr. Leland. Starting with new lodgings," Zoe prompted.

"Yes, yes. Horace, we have an appointment with an agent who will show us several places that may meet the needs of Mr. Leland and his bride," Mr. Love said, bubbling with enthusiasm. "I have told the agent very clearly what you desire—convenient but not deluxe, furnished if possible, rooms for a live-in nurse or housekeeper, plenty of natural light and a garden." Mr. Love pulled a large gold watch from his pocket. "The agent will arrive at the hotel at two o'clock. That gives us time for a pleasant luncheon at a restaurant near here—a favorite of mine. I hope that you will join us, Miss Violet."

Zoe grabbed Vi's arm and demanded, "You will, won't you, Violet? It's a real Roman restaurant, not a place for tourists. And the food is divine! Is it true that Americans eat things like opossums and rattlesnakes? I've read that they do. I have so many questions to ask you about America. Oh, please come with us. Please!"

"Of course Vi will come, Miss Love," Horace said, and Vi saw that he was actually grinning.

She looked at Zoe and said, "My future brother-in-law has instructed me to see Rome, so I guess this is an excellent starting place."

Looping her arm through Vi's, young Zoe declared in her best Italian, "*Che belleza*! How wonderful! But you must not just see Rome. You must hear and feel and taste it. And

I will be your guide if you like. You are my first ever American friend in Rome, Violet. Girl friend, I mean, for Papa has many friends who are very kind to me. But I don't know many people of my own age. I shall call you *la bella Violetta*—the beautiful Violet. Oh, we can be friends, can't we?"

In the Streets of Rome

Go out quickly into the streets and alleys of the town and bring in the poor, the crippled, the blind and the lame.

LUKE 14:21

In the Streets of Rome

*T*he next week passed in a whirlwind. Missy and Mrs. O'Flaherty made the move to the boarding house, and under their ministrations — and Mrs. Warden's superb nursing — Lester's recovery was truly underway. By the end of the first week, he was able to leave his bed for a few minutes and sit in a chair — a dizzying yet exhilarating experience for a man whose very survival had been so recently in doubt.

After many tries, Horace and Mr. Love finally found a house suitable for Lester's recuperation. It was a comfortable, furnished *casa* in Mr. Love's own neighborhood. Satisfied that her fiancé could do without her care for a few hours, Missy visited the house and gave her approval, and Horace acquired the lease. Then he began the search for house servants and made arrangements to move Lester to his new home as soon as Dr. Di Marco agreed.

Plans also proceeded for the wedding. Using his considerable influence with the local bureaucracy, Mr. Love was able to cut the usual long wait for a marriage license, but even so, the ceremony could not be scheduled for another two weeks. The minister was found when Mr. Love and Zoe took Horace and Vi to services at the Protestant church they attended. Mr. Love arranged for Horace to meet with the clergyman after the service, and after hearing the situation, the minister readily agreed to officiate.

Vi was kept busy shopping — something she rarely enjoyed — for things Missy would need in the new house. Mrs. O'Flaherty was able to accompany her on these excursions, and Zoe often came as well. They even found time for sightseeing, and Zoe proved to be both enthusiastic and knowledgeable as a tour guide. Somewhat against his better judgment, Horace allowed the two girls to venture out on their own on occasion, and Vi honored his trust by returning to the hotel at the exact times he specified.

"Your grandfather is very nice, but also very strict," Zoe observed one afternoon as she and Vi were walking back to the Hotel Roma after a visit to the Trevi Fountain, where they had tossed coins into the pool and made their wishes.

The sun was high and hot, and both girls carried parasols to protect them from the burning rays. Many people were out, and Vi heard frequent snatches of conversation in English, German, Spanish, and other languages she didn't recognize. It had just occurred to her that the street was more crowded with tourists than Romans. She had learned about the Mediterranean custom of resting after lunch, and she herself looked forward to a cool drink on the shady terrace as soon as they reached the hotel—though it was much too hot to hurry her pace.

"I can see why you might think him a bit old-fashioned," Vi said in response to Zoe's comment, "but I never think of him as strict. He is doing what he knows my mother would do if she could be here."

"Then your mother is strict?" Zoe asked.

"No, she is careful of our welfare. You've always lived in great cities, Zoe, but I am a country girl. Back at home, I can wander wherever I like so long as I tell Mamma where I will be, and I often go out alone. But my mother and Grandpapa naturally worry about me being on my own in Rome or Paris or even in London, where I was born. I imagine that a person could easily become lost here, and that wouldn't be fun."

"But I will protect you," Zoe said fearlessly, "for I am your friend and I know all about big cities."

Vi laughed at this display of bravado. "I know you do," she said kindly, "and you are an excellent guide. Still, we are young girls, and we cannot anticipate what might happen. I really don't mind following Grandpapa's rules because they make good sense to me."

"Um," Zoe mused, "I do know there are parts of the city where Papa will not allow me to go, even with him. So your grandfather is probably being wise after all. And as I said, he is very nice. He always laughs at my jokes, though I am sure he must think them very silly."

They continued their leisurely walk, passing shops full of luxuries and street vendors selling a great variety of goods. Coming upon one of the city's many piazzas, or squares, Vi saw several large carts loaded with flowers, and she walked over to look at the brilliant display. She had been thinking about a bridal bouquet for Missy, and she wanted to learn what blossoms were available.

Her Italian was good enough for her to tell the vendor that she was "only looking." The great variety of flowers astonished her, and Zoe explained that this bounty of colors and fragrances came from all parts of Italy and other countries as well.

"Do you know the language of flowers?" Zoe asked.

When Vi confessed that she did not, Zoe explained that each flower has a hidden meaning. "It is symbolic," Zoe said, "a way for people to communicate without using words. I learned it from a governess I had once. She was English and the language of flowers is very popular there, especially among couples in love. The English are very proper in their conduct, she said, and they use flowers to say what they are not supposed to say in person. It is a very pretty custom, I guess, but I cannot imagine not speaking my mind."

She pointed to a container of red rosebuds, giggling, "Those are for us, *Violetta*—pure and lovely. And that iris means 'a message.' "

They spent some time looking at the flowers, with Zoe explaining the meaning of each. Then Zoe went to examine some bunches of wildflowers and herbs while Vi's attention was caught by a bouquet of white roses. Vi moved away from her companion to look at the roses. As she leaned over to smell their rich, cool scent, she felt something beside her—a swift movement near her arm, over which her small purse was hanging. Instinctively, she reached out and spun around. She found herself holding the thin wrist of a small, dark-haired boy in a clean but tattered shirt and short pants, and the surprise in his face was no less than her own.

Zoe, hurrying to Vi, shouted at the boy, "You awful little thief! Did you think you could steal my friend's purse? We will call the police—*polizia*—and they will teach you a lesson!"

The boy's eyes were like saucers filled with dark fear. He yanked his arm to free himself, but Vi held on. Then she became aware that the vendor, too, was yelling, and several curious bystanders were gathering around the scene. Vi had no idea what the angry vendor was saying, but the look in the boy's eyes told her that the words must be threats.

From the corner of her eye, Vi saw a tall figure in a uniform pushing his way authoritatively through the onlookers. Without thinking, she let go of the boy. He had been pulling away from her, and when she loosened her grip, he spun around to run. But he was caught off-balance and tripped. Vi held out her hand to help him steady himself, but he stumbled backwards and fell, and Vi knew that her gesture had only frightened him more.

Before she could make another move, she saw the boy literally lifted from the ground, the collar of his shabby shirt held in the large hand of the policeman.

The boy, whom Vi guessed to be no more than seven or eight years old, had begun to cry, and he was muttering something. But Vi couldn't hear him for all the excited conversations going on around her.

Her Italian was just good enough for her to make out the general meanings. Zoe was telling the policeman that the boy was a thief—had tried to steal her friend's purse. The policeman was saying something about places for beggars and thieves. The vendor was yelling about urchins and gypsies and jails!

The words came out of Vi's mouth without any conscious thought. "*Silenzio!*" she shouted about the din. "Please, everyone, be quiet now!"

To her astonishment, everyone did fall silent. Vi bent down to the boy and at last could understand what he was saying: "Mamma, Mamma, Mamma," over and over.

"Tell the policeman and the flower seller that we are fine," Vi commanded Zoe. "Tell them that we will handle this. Nothing was stolen. It was a misunderstanding. Please, Zoe, tell them to go away."

Zoe, responding to Vi's unyielding tone, addressed the two men. Fearful of losing a customer, the vendor backed away. Though the tall policeman still held the child by the collar, Vi took the boy's hand gently in her own and spoke to him soothingly. "Don't worry. You're all right. We'll find your mother."

She looked up at Zoe. "Ask the policeman to please let him go," she said. "Tell him there is no problem—*non problema*."

Zoe did as she was told, rattling off a barrage of Italian that Vi could not comprehend. The policeman was clearly reluctant to release his little prisoner, but Zoe persisted, and finally the officer freed the boy.

Vi fully expected the child to run, but he didn't.

Still holding his thin hand, Vi asked, "Do you know English?"

He nodded and answered in a tiny voice, "Yes, *signorina*, a little."

"You will run away?"

"No, *signorina*. Only run from police."

"Then let's talk," she said. "I see a bench over there where we can sit."

By now, the curious onlookers had sensed that the little drama was over and were moving on. Zoe spoke a little more with the policeman, then he also went on his way. The seller, who had actually seen the boy attempt to grab Vi's purse, leaned against one of his carts—sulking but silent.

Stroking the boy's hand lightly and still speaking to him in gentle words and tone, Vi finally stood up and led him to the seat nearby. They sat down, with Zoe standing close by, and Vi said, "I don't think you are really a thief, but maybe you needed something from my purse."

The boy bowed his head. He couldn't look at her when he said, "I need coins. Money. For food."

"But it is wrong to steal," Vi said evenly. "Did you know that?"

"Yes, *signorina*. It is in the Bible. Stealing is wrong."

"And do you believe the Bible?"

160

The little head popped up, and two bright, dark, tear-filled eyes met her gaze. "Yes, I believe. God will punish me because I steal."

"He will forgive you if you ask His pardon. He loves you, and He wants you to be good."

The boy blinked several times, and with his free hand, he wiped roughly at his eyes. "I'm sorry," he said with a sniffle. "You are a nice lady. I'm sorry to you and sorry to God."

"Then He forgives you, and so do I," Vi said with a smile. "Tell me, what is your name?"

"Alberto."

"And I am Violet—*Violetta*." Beckoning to Zoe, Vi added, "And this is my friend Zoe. She's sorry that she yelled at you, but she was afraid for me. Weren't you, Zoe?"

The younger girl, who was not at all sorry for her behavior, nevertheless nodded in agreement. The boy smiled at her, and Zoe, who had a city dweller's mistrust of street children, felt her heart melt a bit at his cherubic face. In spite of herself, Zoe asked, "Do you want food because you are hungry—*affamato*?"

The boy sat straighter and said, "Not hungry. Food for *Mamma*, my mother. And *sorella mia*?" He looked confused, so Zoe said, "Your sister."

"I would like to give you money for your mother and sister," Vi said, "but you must do two things for me first. You must promise that you will take the money to your mother so that she can buy the food you need. Will you do that?"

"*Si*. Yes, *Signorina Violetta*. I promise."

"And you must come have something to eat with my friend and me," she said.

Seeing his face darken, she added, "Just a little something, for I know you are not really hungry. I want to hear more about your mother and sister, and we can have a little snack while we talk."

"I eat," the boy agreed, "just a little."

A few minutes later, they were all sitting in an outdoor café. Vi ordered tea and cakes for Zoe and herself and a hearty sandwich and milk for their companion. The waiter cast a suspicious eye at the boy in the ragged clothes, but Vi said, "Alberto is our guest, and I want him to have your best ham and cheese."

The waiter, shaking his head at the strange behavior of the young lady, did as he was bid. Before he returned with the food and drink, Vi discovered that the boy had learned English from his father, a sailor who had died in an accident at sea the year before. His mother had taken work as a cook for a well-to-do family, but the family had moved to an Alpine region several months ago and the boy's mother had been unable to find another job. Alberto had never been to school because he looked after his younger sister while his mother had worked. Now he prowled the streets and markets of the city, begging for money and searching for food.

When his sandwich was set before him, Alberto dove into it with such abandon that Vi realized it may have been a day or more since he last ate. She and Zoe silently sipped their tea, allowing the child to enjoy his meal. And when the sandwich and milk were gone, Vi ordered more milk and passed the sweet cakes to Alberto. She also asked the waiter to pack a box of food—ordering meats, cheese, fruit, bread, and butter for Alberto's family. And finally she asked the waiter to summon a carriage.

When the boy could eat no more, he scooted his frail body back in his chair, grinned disarmingly, and said, "*Grazia*, Miss *Violetta*. *Grazia*, Miss Zoo-ee."

"Thank you, Alberto, for being our guest," Vi said. "Now, we will escort you home."

———

"Oh, I wish you could have seen Vi, Mr. Dinsmore," Zoe was saying excitedly. They were dining at the Loves' favorite restaurant, and before they were even seated, Zoe had told her father and Horace about the Constanza family and what had happened in the piazza that afternoon.

"Vi was like a—a general commanding his troops. When she shouted *silenzio*, everyone stopped talking. Even the policeman! And the whole time that she was telling me what to say, Vi was being so kind and gentle with Alberto. Oh, Papa, everybody did just what she said. And because I was translating for her," she added with a giggle, "they did what I said, too."

"You did that child a great favor," Mr. Love said to Vi.

"But you took a great risk, my dear," Horace said sternly. "You girls should not have taken the boy to his home by yourselves."

"That is not the worst part of the city, but it is not a safe neighborhood," Mr. Love agreed. "Zoe, you should have known better."

Before Zoe could defend herself, Vi said, "Zoe did warn me, Mr. Love, but I insisted. I wanted to come back here and wait for you and Grandpapa, but Alberto was so anxious to get home to his mother and sister with the food we bought. I was afraid for him to go alone, because that box was a tempting target for others to steal. I was so glad that Zoe was with me. She was able to tell the carriage driver the quickest way to Alberto's street and to translate for me in our conversation with his mother."

"Well, let us hope the food and money are received in the same spirit they were given," Mr. Love said. "Rome is plagued with these street urchins and even the youngest can be very skilled thieves and connivers."

"Alberto is not like that, Papa," Zoe said adamantly. "I don't think he had ever tried to steal before because he was not very good at it. His mother, Mrs. Constanza, seemed a very nice woman. She was so upset that her son might be stealing money, and very grateful to us for bringing him home. And the little sister was so adorable, Papa. You know that I'm not very trusting, Papa, but I really believe that they are good people in misfortune."

"Where is the father?" Horace asked.

"Killed, Mr. Dinsmore, in a sea accident. I asked Mrs. Constanza about it, and she said that he was a merchant sailor, not a navy seaman," Zoe said. "Does that make a difference?"

"It would explain why the family was left in poverty," Horace said thoughtfully. "It's very unlikely that she receives any kind of pension. There is charity, of course."

"She is a proud woman," Vi said. "She told us that she works at her church when she can, in exchange for the charity they provide, but she wants a job so that she can support her children and send them to school."

Horace glanced at Mr. Love. "I wonder if we might be of some help," he said.

"If she is a good cook, and as honest as the girls believe. . ." Mr. Love began, then left his thought unfinished.

"A cook for Missy and Lester!" Vi exclaimed. "Oh, might that be possible, Grandpapa?"

"I would want to meet with your Mrs. Constanza, of course," Horace replied. "And we would need to investigate the family a little more."

"I can manage that," Mr. Love volunteered. "I should be able to contact the people for whom she worked."

"And Missy and Lester must agree," Horace added. "There are rooms enough in the new house for the family, but I'm not sure that Missy and Lester are prepared to have small children around during this stage of Lester's recuperation."

Vi started to say that she was sure her sister and Lester would agree, but she held back. The decision must be theirs, and she had no right to jump to conclusions. *Be patient*, she told herself firmly.

"I think we should learn more before we mention this to Missy," Horace was saying. "Mitchell, can you accompany me tomorrow on a visit to the Constanzas?"

"Do you remember their address?" Mr. Love asked his daughter.

"I do, Papa. It is a very poor neighborhood, so you must be watchful when you go there," Zoe replied with great earnestness.

"We shall, my dear," Mr. Love promised with a loving smile. "Thank you for worrying about us. Perhaps you can understand now why I worry about you."

Zoe's lovely face registered her astonishment. "I hadn't thought about it that way, Papa," she declared. "But you're right. I worry about you because I love you. And you worry about me because you love me."

"And someday, my darling, you will have children, and you will worry about them because you love them so much that their welfare is more important to you than even your own life and happiness," Mr. Love said softly.

Zoe reached over and laid her hand on her father's. She smiled brilliantly and said, "I will try to be less headstrong, Papa, because I don't want you to worry."

It was a lovely moment between father and daughter, and soon over. But Vi had noticed a look of concern pass swiftly across Mr. Love's pleasant face as he spoke to his daughter. What it signified, she couldn't guess.

CHAPTER

13

Vi's Rome

Anyone who gives you a cup of water in my name because you belong to Christ will certainly not lose his reward.

MARK 9:41

Vi's Rome

hey had been in Rome for almost a month, and looking back, Vi could hardly believe what had been accomplished. Lester was still weak, but he was gaining weight and reclaiming his youthful good looks. He could not only stand now but was taking short walks, and he had begun to work again, sitting on the narrow balcony of the apartment and sketching the small garden behind the boarding house. At Mrs. O'Flaherty's insistence — for she feared Missy was not sleeping well — Missy was again staying at the hotel at night, but she returned to the *pensione* every morning and watched over Lester like a hawk. Vi thought she had never seen her sister so happy.

It had been decided that Mrs. O'Flaherty would remain with the newlyweds until they returned to the United States, while Horace and Vi were scheduled to leave Rome in another week, just a few days after the wedding. Vi was sad to be parting from Mrs. O'Flaherty so soon. But there was good news on another front.

The investigation of Mrs. Constanza had proved more than successful. Through his diplomatic contacts, Mr. Love had located the family for whom she had worked and received a glowing recommendation of both her cooking skills and her reliability. He had also spoken with the Constanzas' parish priest, learning more about the family's sad history and Mrs. Constanza's devotion to her church.

From the moment she first laid eyes on Alberto and his sister, Angelina, there had been no doubt that Missy would welcome the Constanzas into her life and her heart. She said that having the children live at the house would make the place seem more like her own home. Lester was no less taken with the children, and he was very impressed with Mrs. Constanza—as was the toughest critic of all, Mrs. O'Flaherty.

So Mrs. Constanza was hired, and she and her children were already in residence at what everyone now called "the Villa Leland." Vi visited them nearly every day, in the company of Mrs. O'Flaherty, who was now overseeing the preparation of the house, and Vi's affection for the children grew every time she saw them.

"How many families are there, who live as the Constanzas did?" Vi asked Mrs. O'Flaherty one morning as they were being driven to the hotel after their visit to the villa.

"More than can be counted," Mrs. O'Flaherty replied. "They live in every city of every land in every corner of this world. And for the most part, they are good people ground down by poverty that is not their fault. At least, that is my experience. Alberto and Angelina are fortunate. Imagine what would have happened if Alberto had tried to steal the purse of someone whose heart was hard. He might have been torn away from his family and sentenced to an institution or prison where he would have learned to be a true criminal. It happens all the time." Then she added, "Jesus loves the poor, but how many of us can say the same?"

"When I first—ah—met Alberto," Vi said thoughtfully, "I guess that I realized he was poor, but I just saw a frightened little boy. Then later, I remembered a time when I was really young and frightened like that. I was lost, and I didn't know what to do. So I just prayed as hard as I could for my Papa to find me, and God answered my prayer. When I looked into Alberto's eyes, maybe I saw myself so alone and scared. I didn't really think about it, Mrs. O. I just wanted to protect him."

"And isn't that what Jesus commanded us to do?" Mrs. O'Flaherty said. "To treat others as we want to be treated."

Vi decided to bring up something that she had been thinking about a great deal, ever since her visit to the Carpenters' mission in New Orleans the year before. "In Psalm 82," she said, "God tells the rulers: 'Defend the cause of the weak and fatherless; maintain the rights of the poor and oppressed. Rescue the weak and needy; deliver them from the hand of the wicked.' But how can we do that? I mean, how can I do that? There are so many children like Alberto. Where do we start to help them all?"

"We start where you did—with one person in need."

"But that's so frustrating," Vi said with a sigh. "If I could help a different person every day for the rest of my life, it would be like a drop in the ocean."

Mrs. O'Flaherty smiled in an odd way and said, "Never underestimate the power of one good act, my girl. You help someone, and the day will come when that person has the opportunity to help another. That is how the lesson of service is spread. Of course, not everyone wants to be helped and there are some who resent good deeds. There are also those who mask evil motives behind the appearance of caring in order to decieve the poor. But we cannot let the occasional rotten apple spoil the barrel, can we?"

"You're saying that we must be prepared for times when our efforts fail," Vi commented.

"Prepared, yes," Mrs. O'Flaherty agreed. "We must also not allow ourselves to become disheartened when our offers of help are rejected. It's a complicated business—dealing with other people—but that is what makes life so very interesting."

Violet's Amazing Summer

Vi slumped against her seat and fell silent. *Life is a very complicated business*, she said to herself, *but God does not give us more than we can handle, does He?*

She sat up and turned to Mrs. O'Flaherty. "I think I understand what you said, Mrs O, about being prepared," she said. "We have to be ready for challenges, don't we? With God in our hearts, we *are* ready for whatever happens. And that includes failures as well as successes. Good things, bad things, sad things—when we trust God, we are ready. Life should be an adventure. That's what Aunt Wealthy said. She said that life's not a tea party. It's a wonderful adventure, even at its hardest. She told me that just before we left Lansdale. She said, 'Trust God, love one another, and live the adventure.' I thought she meant our journey to Rome, but she was talking about an adventure of the spirit, wasn't she? Oh, I know now that is what she meant!"

Mrs. O'Flaherty nodded in agreement. Then she began to laugh, for she had been infected by Vi's excitement. And Vi laughed, too.

Vi soon found herself with more hours to enjoy Rome, and she thought of the city now as part of her great adventure. For the first time on the trip, she opened her senses—seeing, hearing, smelling, and tasting the city, just as Zoe had said. Vi drank in its brilliance and history, but also saw its darker shadows—the poor and hungry and homeless. Rome opened her eyes; for the first time in her life, Vi looked at the strangers she passed on the street and saw with crystal clarity how astonishing God's creation really is, in all its variations.

Vi's Rome

She purchased a small sketch pad and pencils and began to draw what she saw. But instead of landscapes, which had always been her subject, Vi worked to capture faces: the waiter at the Loves' favorite restaurant who was always so jolly but had sad eyes. The policeman Vi saw every afternoon on her walks—the very same one who had nabbed Alberto at the flower stall. The middle-aged and expensively dressed American lady who spoke to no one and always ate alone in the hotel dining room. The sharp-eyed children who begged for money and, Vi observed, picked the pockets of unsuspecting tourists at the famous Spanish Steps. Each face was, to Vi, like the cover of a book, and inside each book were stories she longed to read. She knew that her sketches weren't very good and showed them to no one except Zoe; Vi's pleasure lay in the effort.

During her explorations of the city, Vi spent a great deal of time with Zoe, and her fondness for the younger girl grew every day. Zoe was, as Horace had said, undisciplined, but there was little willfulness in her independence. As the girls began to know each other better, Vi realized that Zoe's bright chatter and assertiveness hid greater depths. In truth, Zoe was shy and not nearly so self-assured as she pretended. She was intelligent and quick-witted, but poorly schooled, and Vi discovered that Zoe was embarrassed by her lack of formal education. But her knowledge was extensive, as Vi learned during their frequent sightseeing ventures. Zoe knew the history of every ancient structure they visited, from the mighty ruins of the Colosseum to the exquisite Pantheon, and she had a storyteller's gift for infusing dry facts with life. So Vi made a new friend, and Zoe became as precious to her as Katie and Abby and all the girls she had come to know in Lansdale.

Each night before bed, Vi wrote to her loved ones at home—detailed letters to her mother and shorter but no less informative communications to Ed. She also wrote Aunt Wealthy and her new friends in Lansdale, thanking them for their hospitality and expressing her hope to see them all again soon.

Meanwhile she and the others waited anxiously for letters from home, and they were finally rewarded when two thick envelopes arrived from Ion. Elsie had written one letter to Missy and another to Horace and Vi. In both, she had expressed her heartfelt approval of the marriage plans and her prayers for Lester's swift recovery. Missy had cried when she read her mother's gentle words of blessing and encouragement. "I am the happiest mother in the world," Elsie wrote at the conclusion of her letter. "I ask only that you send me a telegram and tell me of the day and hour of your marriage, so that I may be with you, in my heart, as you pledge your love for each other and affirm your devotion to our Lord and Savior. Begin your life together in joy, my dears, and know that you have all our love. . . Mamma."

Other letters came—from Rose and Trip and Ed and from Lester's aunt and uncle at Fairview, who conveyed their family's best wishes and love. A delightful epistle arrived in the unmistakable hand of Aunt Wealthy. Near the end, she included a special message for Missy and Lester: "I've never been married, as you know, but over my one hundred years of spinsterhood, I've seen many good wives and good husbands weather their ups and downs and downs and ups. And I think I understand their secret. Always be kind to one another, and you cannot stumble in the potholes life creates for us. My wedding gift to you is from God's Holy Word: 'Love is patient, love is kind.' My hand is too unsteady to write out the rest, but you know it in your hearts. 'Love never fails.' "

When Lester read Wealthy's letter, he said, "Your aunt has given us a wonderful gift, Missy. Might we use it in our ceremony?"

Missy agreed instantly. The text for their marriage service would be the thirteenth chapter of 1 Corinthians.

CHAPTER 14

Two Become One

The man said, "This is now bone of my bones and flesh of my flesh."

GENESIS 2:23

Two Become One

*O*n the morning before the wedding, the family gathered early in Lester's apartment. In just a few hours, Lester would be safely in his new home, and on the very next day, he would become a husband.

If Missy had had her way, she and Lester would have been married much earlier, when the marriage license was finally received. But Lester had set one condition. He was determined to stand by her side when they made their vows and to walk with her as husband and wife. He worked very hard at increasing his strength and stamina, and Missy was so proud of his efforts that she could hardly begrudge him the extra days needed to achieve his goal.

When all his possessions were removed and his rooms stood empty, Lester confided to Missy that he felt a little sad leaving the apartment and the neighborhood he had come to know so well. But after he had walked down the flights of creaking stairs, bid farewell to his pleasant landlady, and stepped out onto the cobbled street, Lester's first reaction was to quote a simple line of verse from Psalm 146: "The LORD sets prisoners free...."

Dr. Di Marco, who had arrived to accompany Lester on the trip to the villa, overheard. "Our beloved Father has indeed freed you from the prison of grave illness," the good doctor said. "And you must show your gratitude by minding your health and following my orders. I do not want you to confound His purpose by taking any foolish chances. That applies to you as well, Miss Travilla," he added, turning to address Missy.

"I'll take very good care of him," Missy responded.

"I have no doubt of that," Dr. Di Marco said, "but you must also care for yourself. A good nurse knows her limits, my dear. I shall not be seeing you so often now, but I have asked Mrs. Warden to stop by your new home every few days. Is that agreeable?"

"More than agreeable, sir," Lester said. "But we will see you tomorrow at the wedding, won't we? You and your wife? We want to meet *Signora* Di Marco, and I owe her an apology for taking you away from her so often during my illness."

"Of course," the doctor said gaily. "We have been through much together, and I would not miss the happy ending. Now, let me help you into the carriage. It is time for you to be on your way."

Mrs. O'Flaherty and Mrs. Constanza had done a wonderful job of readying "the Villa Leland." Horace had hired several cleaners, and the fine house had been dusted and polished from top to bottom—including the magnificently delicate crystal chandeliers that adorned the entry, the main parlor, and the dining room. The house had recently been renovated to include all the necessary conveniences. But its most important feature was a large sunroom that opened onto a broad stone terrace and the rear garden. The sunroom, with its soaring glass windows, would become Lester's new studio. And the lush garden, which was maintained to perfection by an irascible man who apparently came with the lease, would be the site of the wedding.

Two Become One

After seeing that Lester was comfortably settled in and issuing a few directions to Mrs. O'Flaherty, Dr. Di Marco insisted that everyone else should depart and allow his patient to rest.

Missy smiled at Dr. Di Marco. "But may I not pamper him just a bit longer?"

The doctor chuckled. "A bit? Of course! We men rely on our wives for a little pampering when the world treats us harshly. But too much pampering will spoil your Lester."

"Just a few minutes, I promise," Missy said. "You've been so good to us, and I hope you will remain our friend as well as our physician."

Dr. Di Marco smiled and made a small bow. "I am honored to be both, Miss Travilla. It will give me great pleasure to be the friend of the new Mr. and Mrs. Leland."

While Horace escorted the physician to his carriage, Missy dutifully followed doctor's orders. She went to Lester, shared sweet words of parting, and kissed him gently. Still, she was tempted to linger, but Vi would hear no excuses.

Hurrying into the parlor, where Lester rested on a brocade chaise and Missy sat beside him, Vi said jokingly, "Lester, you're going to have to make her leave. You're the master of the house now. Be masterful, and shoo her out."

Missy stood, reluctantly, as Vi tapped her foot in mock impatience.

"It's past three o'clock," Vi said, "and the dressmaker is waiting. If you want to have your wedding dress tomorrow, we must leave now."

"You sound just like Papa," Missy laughed as she finally let go of Lester's hand.

Missy bent, gave him a quick kiss on the forehead, and said softly, "I will see you tomorrow, my love."

Violet's Amazing Summer

Some twenty hours later, at the precise time that Horace Dinsmore was standing beside his granddaughter before the minister in the resplendent garden of the house in Rome, his own wife and daughter were sitting in Elsie's bedroom at Ion. Chloe was with them, and all three women were dressed in their nightgowns and robes.

"The rooster just barely had time to crow here," Chloe said, "and to think, it's already midday over there in Italy, and our Missy's getting herself married right this minute. I'm sure glad you got that telegram, Elsie, so we can share the moment. This world's an amazing thing, isn't it? All God's creation is mighty amazing."

"Indeed it is," Elsie agreed. "I thank you both for joining me this morning. It's early for a wedding, but I wanted to celebrate. God is blessing me with a new son at this very hour, and I couldn't have slept through it."

"You sad not to be there?" asked Chloe.

"A little, I suppose," Elsie said, "but hardly enough to notice. Since Missy's first letter arrived, I have been so sure that her decision was the right one that I've not worried at all. I'd have liked to be there, but to make the journey would have delayed their plans. I trust Papa and Vi to bring us a full account."

Rose passed teacups to the others and said, "I propose a toast to them all, and ask the Lord's blessings on our Missy and Lester and all who love and cherish them."

The three took sips of their tea. Then Elsie bowed her head as she prayed: "Heavenly Father, You have been so generous to us—restoring Lester and bringing him and Missy together on this day. Please extend Your loving hands now to Papa and Vi as they begin their journey home to us. Watch over them and keep them safe. Amen."

Rose and Chloe shared her prayer for the travelers who would soon be returning.

"Well, Miss Elsie," Chloe said after a few moments. "Who's gonna be next? You think Mr. Ed will find himself a bride anytime soon?"

Before Elsie could answer, Rose said, "Dear me, where is my head? I meant to tell you last night, Elsie, but we were so busy talking about the wedding that it completely slipped my mind."

"What, Mamma?" Elsie asked.

Rose smiled and said, "The answer to Chloe's question. The next wedding in the family will be that of Isa Conley and James Keith. It is all settled, and the marriage is to be in early December."

A look of comic skepticism came to Chloe's face. "Does Miss Louise know about this? She's been holding out against those two lovebirds, just as stubborn as an old mule."

"Well, she has given her consent now," Rose said. "When I saw her yesterday, she spoke most graciously of James and his family. She even suggested that his father might perform the ceremony."

"But whatever finally convinced her?" Elsie wondered.

"Your Papa," Rose replied with a warm smile. "Horace can be quite clever. You know how fond he is of Isa, and he couldn't imagine a better match than James. But he knew not to try to force his opinion on Louise. Horace was even somewhat understanding of her fear for Isa's future if she married a poor clergyman. So he decided to remove Louise's objection entirely — 'make it a moot point,' he said.

Just before sailing for Europe, he arranged with his New York lawyer to establish a generous trust fund for Isa, with the money available upon her marriage. Isa received notification of the trust several days ago. She came straight to see me and protested that she couldn't accept such a large gift. But I assured her that my darling husband would be heartbroken if she refused. Besides, she and James never have to use the money unless there is a need. I suggested she think of it as a trust for her children and grandchildren and their futures. Isa finally agreed, and when she told her mother, all of Louise's worries simply melted away. Isa telegraphed James at Viamede, he replied immediately, and so the wedding is on. I sent a telegram to Horace, so hopefully the good news will soon be known to all our loved ones in Rome."

"That Mr. Horace can be a sly fox," Chloe chortled. "Looks like the fox has outwitted the old mule this time!"

Amid the laughter, Rose looked into the teapot. Quickly distributing the last of the hot drink, she said, "Let us raise our cups once more, in honor of Isa and James."

"And Louise, as the mother of the bride-to-be," Elsie added.

Serious now, Chloe said, "God bless them all, and forgive me for makin' fun of Miss Louise. Maybe the happiness of Miss Isa's wedding will open a crack in her heart, and the good Lord can slip in there and wash away her bitterness and fear. I'm praying that Miss Louise will forget about being hard and angry for just a minute or two, 'cause that's all the time it takes to feel the healing Spirit and know the saving grace of our Lord."

The women sat in companionable silence for some time. Then the clock on the mantel chimed the half hour, and

Elsie said, "It is too bad that the tea is finished, for now you could toast me." A beautiful smile lit her face as she added, "If the clock is correct, I am now a mother-in-law."

Across the ocean, thousands of miles from Elsie's room, the same sun that was rising over the hills at Ion stood at its full height above Rome. Lester Leland stood beside Missy, lifted the simple veil from her radiant face, and bent to kiss his new bride. Then Vi returned the bouquet of white roses to her sister, and the new Mr. and Mrs. Lester Leland walked forward to greet their guests.

CHAPTER

15

A Final Request

*Do not be afraid, little flock,
for your Father has been
pleased to give you
the kingdom.*

LUKE 12:32

A Final Request

*H*ow is it possible to feel so many emotions, Grandpapa?" Vi asked, shaking her head in consternation.

She and Horace were having breakfast on the balcony of their hotel suite. It was their last meal in Rome, for their train would leave at midday.

"What do you mean, dear?"

"I'm excited to be going home. I can hardly wait to hug Mamma and Grandmamma and Rosemary and the boys and to see everyone at Ion and The Oaks and Roselands. I feel as if I've been away for years. But I'm so sad about leaving Missy and Lester here. And I'm already missing Mrs. O'Flaherty and Zoe and Mr. Love. I feel as if I might never see them again. I want to laugh and cry at the same time! I almost want to stamp my foot and have a baby tantrum because I can't be with everyone."

Vi set her fork down on her plate with a loud click. "Do you know what this is like, Grandpapa?" she said. At his puzzled look, she continued, "It's like reading a book full of exciting adventure and romance and scary parts, too. And you get to the very last chapter, and the book is suddenly taken away. And then you never know the ending! All you can do is worry if everything turns out the way you expect. Or did the author have a last surprise that you'll never know?"

"That is the difference between books and real life, dearest, but believe me, I understand your frustration," Horace said gently. "In life, few things ever turn out quite as we expect. We have been living so intensely these past weeks and months—Lansdale and the reunion with the Keiths,

189

the news of Lester's illness, our trip here, our fears for Lester, his recovery and then the wedding, the excitement of this great city. It is hard to calm ourselves down and slow our pace. It is hard to let go and allow the people we love to get on with their lives without our help."

"I'm just being silly, wanting to go home and wanting to stay here and wanting to know everything about everybody," Vi said with a sigh.

"Sometimes we need to take a rest from wanting, even when all we want is good things for those we love," Horace said. "I don't mean that we stop caring. But sometimes we need to sit back and simply experience the world God has given us. We need to breathe the pure air, and smell the sweetness of the fresh grass, and observe the people around us. To clear our minds of worry and care and simply listen to God."

"To be like the lilies," Vi said softly. She quoted from the twelfth chapter of Luke: "Consider how the lilies grow. They do not labor or spin. Yet I tell you, not even Solomon in all his splendor was dressed like one of these. If that is how God clothes the grass of the field, which is here today, and tomorrow is thrown into the fire, how much more will he clothe you, O you of little faith!"

Horace smiled at his granddaughter and said, "Worrying can become a bad habit, my girl, like biting your nails. It distracts us from serious thought and positive action."

Then Horace had another thought: "I am quite sure that some of your frustration is born of your fears for Missy — and perhaps also your fear at parting with her. Since you were an infant, you two have always been close. Until your visit to Lansdale, you had rarely been far away from each other for more than a few days. I know that there is often a special bond between sisters."

A Final Request

Vi lowered her head and said softly, "There has been a lot of change all of a sudden, Grandpapa."

She looked up, and Horace saw tears in her eyes.

"You told me once that I wasn't afraid of change, but I don't always like it. I never expected that we'd leave Missy here," Vi said, her voice shaking. "I was getting used to the idea of her marrying in December and leaving Ion. But not living so very far away. It hurts, Grandpapa."

Horace thought of many comforting words, but reflecting quickly on Vi's nature, he said, "Your sadness is natural, and with some time and God's help, you will deal with it. I do not think you need my advice right now. I will just repeat what I said earlier. We all need time to rest our thoughts and gain perspective. Give yourself some time and listen to God. Let Him be your comfort. We all spend so much time asking Him for help, that we often forget how good it feels just to talk with Him."

The tears had receded from Vi's eyes. She sniffed once, and then she smiled. "Thanks, Grandpapa. I think you're right, that I don't need advice. I already know what to do."

Then her smile widened, and the little dimple near her mouth seemed almost to wink. "I'll get over it, but sometimes a girl just needs to let off some steam and you're very good at listening."

Horace rose and came behind her to help her from her chair. "What choice did I have?" he teased. "You threatened to stamp your foot and have a tantrum. And I am much too old to deal with that frightful prospect."

"Did I have tantrums when I was a baby?" Vi asked as she stood up.

"Just the usual number," he said.

"More than Missy?"

"Yes, a few more I'd say. Missy was a particularly placid child."

"More than Rosemary?"

"Oh, no, dear. I believe Rosemary still holds the record for tantrums in your household."

Vi laughed as they walked back into the suite. Horace put his arm around her shoulder and gave her a quick hug.

"It will be so good to see Rosemary again. And all the boys," Vi said cheerfully.

"Does that include Ed?" Horace asked. "He will be meeting us in New York, and I think he would be thoroughly provoked to know that you called him a boy."

Vi laughed again. "Oh, it is good to be going home, Grandpapa."

"Very, very good," he replied.

Vi was in her bedroom packing the last of her things. In the sitting room, Horace was gathering some papers and letters and putting them into his valise, when there was a knock at the door.

Thinking it was a member of the hotel staff, Horace called, "Come in."

The door opened, and Mr. Love entered.

Horace immediately went to his friend. "Mitchell!" he said in a hearty tone. "You are early. I did not expect you for another hour. I really appreciate your seeing us off at the train terminal today."

"I need to speak with you privately," Mr. Love replied, and Horace heard an unfamiliar seriousness in the man's voice.

"What is it?" Horace asked, ushering Mr. Love to a comfortable seat.

Mr. Love's face was more solemn than Horace had ever seen it. The merry smile was gone, and his usually bright eyes were oddly dull.

"I have come to ask a great favor of you," Mr. Love began. "I told you that I retired last year for health reasons."

"Yes," Horace said. "You said that you had had some heart problems, but you gave me the impression that the condition is relatively minor."

"It isn't. I have been under Dr. Di Marco's care since shortly after Zoe and I came here to Rome. I believed that I was merely suffering from stress. The political situation was highly unstable, and I was traveling a great deal on diplomatic assignments. I began experiencing some small discomfort—mostly shortness of breath and fatigue—so I finally went to the doctor, and he found—well, more than a small problem. My heart is giving out on me, Horace. I seem fit enough now, but the end is inevitable."

"But there must be something—" Horace protested.

"There is nothing to be done. I've seen other physicians—specialists who confirm Dr. Di Marco's diagnosis. I will have perhaps another year, if I am careful, but no more."

Mr. Love leaned forward and gripped Horace's knee. "Don't be sad for me, old friend. I have had a good life, and in my small way, I believe I have served my country well. I have few regrets. I don't fear death, for I trust with all my heart that it is but a new beginning. But you must know what does frighten me."

Horace lay his hand over his friend's and felt how cold it was. In a hushed tone, he said, "Zoe."

"She is too young to be left alone, Horace," Mr. Love said. "There are no relatives for her to turn to. I have no family save Zoe herself, and her mother's family are all gone now. There is no one to turn to."

"You have me, Mitchell," Horace said. "And my family. Zoe can come to us whenever you like and be welcomed as family. You can both come. Have you considered returning to the United States before. . ." Horace hesitated.

"I thought of it, but the doctors have made it clear that the journey would be dangerous, and I don't want to gamble with the time I have left. Besides, I'm happy here, and Zoe is happy. I've lived so long in Europe that it is my home. I have many friends who will help us, and they would gladly take Zoe in. But Horace, I want her to discover her native land. She will receive an adequate monetary inheritance, but I would also like to provide her something more precious—the chance to get to know her own country."

Mr. Love paused, and his face brightened. "I have denied my daughter very little," he went on, "and it is perhaps true that I have pampered her to a fault. But I did not give her the one thing that has driven my life—her country. Serving my nation was always my great passion, from boyhood. Yet I denied that same feeling to my daughter. If you could help me give her America. . . well. . ."

"Rest assured that she will have what you desire," Horace said. "When the time comes—and I pray that you have more time than you expect—whenever it comes, Zoe will have a home with us. But Mitchell, does she know of your condition?"

"No, but I must tell her soon," Mr. Love said. "I cannot hide my weakness much longer, and she must be prepared. It will be easier now that I know her future is settled."

"But do you think she will want to come to America?" Horace asked.

Mr. Love pulled at his beard thoughtfully and said, "I believe she will. This visit of yours seems to have had a strong influence on her—especially her friendship with Violet. Your granddaughter is a wonderful young lady, and her acceptance of Zoe has meant a great deal to my child. We have always moved in distinguished circles, as diplomats do, but Zoe has few acquaintances of her own age."

"Vi likes Zoe very much," Horace agreed. "We all do."

"She's a good-hearted girl, but not always easy to manage," Mr. Love said in a warning tone.

"No child is always easy to manage," Horace smiled. "But we have a lot of experience."

"Shouldn't you discuss this with your wife before making a commitment?" Mr. Love asked.

"My dear Mitchell, I know my Rose's heart almost as well as my own. She will be as eager as I to welcome Zoe into our home and our lives."

The two old friends continued to talk for another twenty minutes, and specific plans were made for the sad time when Horace's promise would be redeemed.

When Vi came into the sitting room, announcing that she had finally crammed the very last thing into her carrying case, she found her grandfather and Mr. Love chatting in the way that old and dear friends do—talking of the past.

"Hello, Mr. Love," Vi said in greeting. "I thought Zoe was coming today."

"I expect her at any minute. She had an errand to run and was very mysterious about it. But she would not let you leave us without a personal farewell," Mr. Love said.

Horace stood and drew his watch from his vest pocket. "The hotel porters will be here shortly to collect our luggage, dear. Missy and Mrs. O'Flaherty are meeting us at the terminal in forty-five minutes."

"Then shall we go to the lobby," Mr. Love said in his normal chipper fashion, "and await my wandering child?"

The Stazione Termini rang with a cacophony of sounds, both mechanical and human. The huge station buzzed with comings and goings, as trains arrived from all parts of the continent. Gongs rang and voices proclaimed departures — Lisbon, Paris, Madrid. Vi wondered how many others here felt as reluctant to begin their journeys as she did.

Missy and Mrs. O'Flaherty met the travelers as promised. To everyone's delight, they were accompanied by Lester, who sported a black cane to steady himself. The family and their friends navigated through the crowds and made their way to the platform. Talking loudly to make themselves heard and laughing gaily, they tried to ignore the inevitable moment when good-byes must be said.

"You look most debonair with that walking stick," Horace remarked to Lester.

"I still need some support," Lester explained. "And I can't lean on Missy at all times. But I will be very relieved when I can throw this thing away."

"From the look of you, that day is not far off," Horace said. "Your progress is really splendid, Lester. It will give me great pleasure to report to your aunt and uncle when I return. I will see them as soon as I get back to The Oaks."

Meanwhile, Missy was saying to Vi, "Tell Mamma that we have made plans to return to Ion in late November, assuming that Lester is fully recovered—which he will be, I know. We will be there in time for Isa's wedding."

Vi hugged her sister's waist and said, "I'm going to miss you, Missy. Ion will not be the same without you."

"Don't think of our absence, darling, but rather our homecoming. November is not so long to wait," Missy said. "You must promise to write me and tell me everything that you and Rosemary and the boys are doing—even their mischief. And promise me that you will watch over Mamma. With Ed at school and me here, you are the eldest Travilla child at home now."

"I know," Vi said, "and I will try to do everything that you would."

"Dearest Vi," Missy said, her voice breaking slightly. "I have never told you what a wonderful sister you are, but I thank God that you're my sister—my strong, smart, loving, wise little sister. I love you, Vi."

Vi was too choked with emotion to say anything. She wrapped her arms around Missy and they embraced, clinging to each other as if they might never again be so close. They did not even hear the train conductor's last call for passengers to board.

"Come, dear girls, it is time," Horace said gently, and his two granddaughters reluctantly broke their embrace. There were only moments left for one last round of hugs and kisses and tearful farewells. Even Mrs. O'Flaherty was crying when she embraced Vi and said, "I will see you in November, my girl, if the good Lord is willing. And we will have more stories to tell one another. Don't you worry about your sister and Mr. Leland. I'll take good care of them."

"I know you will, Mrs. O," Vi said tearfully. "I know you will."

She wanted to say more, but Horace had taken her arm and was pushing her toward the train. The conductor was polite but clearly impatient to get them aboard.

Mr. Love and Zoe had been standing a little apart from the family, reluctant to intrude on their last few minutes together. Unnoticed by anyone in the hurry of leaving the hotel and meeting at the station, a small paper package nestled in the crook of Zoe's arm. But as Vi stepped up to the train carriage, Zoe ran forward and shoved the package into her friend's hand.

"These are for you," Zoe called over the whistle and roar of the train. "From the place we found Alberto."

The train began to move, and the grinding of metal on metal as the wheels turned on the track almost drowned out Zoe's last words. She was running now, trying to keep up with the train's gathering speed.

"Don't forget me, Vi! I'll never forget you!" she shouted. The others caught up to her, and they all stood in a tight bunch, waving and shouting words that Vi could not hear.

Vi leaned out over the carriage door, waving furiously at her loved ones and trying to capture their images in her mind, but as the train gathered speed, Horace drew her into their compartment and raised the window. Still she stared back toward the station, hoping to catch one more glimpse of those she was leaving behind.

Finally, she sat down next to Horace, and he took a handkerchief from his pocket and dabbed gently at her wet cheeks.

"What do you have there?" he asked, motioning at the little paper sack in Vi's hand.

Vi opened the sack and withdrew a small bouquet.

"They're violets, Grandpapa, blue violets," she said. "From Zoe."

"What a sweet gift. Violets for our *Violetta*."

"But do you know what they mean, Grandpapa? Zoe told me all about the language of flowers, the meanings that each flower symbolizes."

"Ah, yes," Horace said. "It is not a language that I speak fluently, though I know that roses are the flower of love and I believe that daisies speak of innocence. But what is the meaning of these pretty violets?"

Vi ran her fingers lightly over the velvety petals of the little flowers and thought how each one looked like a face. This made her think again of the faces of the ones she had just left behind and of those she would soon be seeing again after so long an absence.

"Blue violets mean faithfulness, Grandpapa," she said. "The faithfulness of friends and family no matter how far away they are. And the faithfulness of God to all who love Him."

Vi looked up into her grandfather's face. She saw in his warm eyes a pensive expression that she attributed to his own bittersweet feelings about leaving Missy and Lester and the others.

"Zoe was sending a message with these violets, that she will be a faithful friend," Vi said softly. "I can't help wondering if I shall ever see her again. Will we ever come back to Rome?"

"I am sure we will," Horace replied. He put his arm around her shoulder and thought about the confidence he had received just that morning from his own dear friend, Mitchell Love.

199

Violet's Amazing Summer

"I am very sure that you will see Zoe again," he said as Vi lay her head against his shoulder and the train hurried them forward on their journey home.

Will Vi ever see Zoe again?
What new dilemmas of the heart lie ahead?
What is true, and who will prove false?

Violet's story continues in:

VIOLET'S TURNING POINT

Book Three
of the
A Life of Faith:
Violet Travilla Series

Collect all of our Elsie products!

A Life of Faith: Elsie Dinsmore Series

* Now Available as a Dramatized Audiobook!